Lucy Diamond lives in Bath with her husband and their three children. When she isn't slaving away on a new book (ahem) you can find her on Twitter @LDiamondAuthor or on Facebook www.facebook.com/LucyDiamondAuthor

A Baby at the Beach Café

Lucy Diamond

PAN BOOKS

First published 2016 by Pan Books
an imprint of Pan Macmillan
20 New Wharf Road, London N1 9RR
Associated companies throughout the world
www.panmacmillan.com

ISBN 978-1-4472-7833-7

Printed and bound by CPI Group (UK) Ltd, Croydon, CR0 4YY

Visit **www.panmacmillan.com** to read more about all our books
and to buy them. You will also find features, author interviews and
news of any author events, and you can sign up for e-newsletters
so that you're always first to hear about our new releases.

A story doesn't come to life until it has a reader. This one's for you.

Chapter One
Evie

'Evie? What on earth are you doing?'

I was lying on the bathroom floor, poking the feather duster up the radiator – that was what I was doing. Now thirty-five weeks pregnant, I had taken to nesting in a big way. I could not be in the kitchen for ten seconds without scrubbing something. I could not walk past a cushion without plumping it up. After a lifetime of avoiding chores, my hormones had turned me into a domestic maniac.

I turned my head to peer up at my husband. 'I'm cleaning,' I said.

He pulled a face that said, *Evie Gray, you are nuts*. He had a point, to be honest. This new obsession had taken me by surprise, too. 'And you're lying on the floor like that because . . . ?' he asked.

'Because it's easier to get to all the low bits,' I told him. My belly was so wide and round these

1

days, it was impossible to bend over. Even kneeling felt like hard work. Besides, I was so tired that I would take any excuse to lie down.

After two years together, and nine weeks of marriage, Ed knew how stubborn I could be. He also knew better than to argue with a crazy pregnant lady. 'Love, I'm not sure you need to clean behind the *radiator*,' he began saying. 'It's probably fine as it is . . .'

I ignored him and gave the feather duster another push. Then came a jingling sound and something fell down onto the floor. *Ha!*

'What's that?' asked Ed.

I hauled myself into a sitting position to take a closer look. It seemed to be a tangle of dusty frayed string, driftwood and sea shells. A memory flashed into my mind. I remembered being a child here in north Cornwall, back when the Beach Café belonged to my Aunty Jo. We had stayed here with her in this very flat, above the café, for week after glorious week every summer. Hot blue-sky days. Sandy feet. The joy of run-ning at full pelt into the foaming waves. And these same shells jingling, up in the bathroom window.

'It's a mobile,' I said. 'I remember it from when I was a kid. It made lovely clinking sounds when there was a breeze.' I carefully picked up the largest strip of wood to show him. There were five strings attached to it, each with dangling shells knotted on. The very sight made me feel as if I was eight years old again, gazing up at it as I played with boats in the bath.

Jo had died two years ago, sadly, leaving me the café in her will. I had taken a chance and moved down here to keep the café going. The first summer was a huge learning curve, but then I hired Ed as my chef, and everything became a million times better. We fell in love, and made a big success of the café together. The flat above the café was our happy little home now, and I couldn't imagine being anywhere else. Once in a while, though, something of Jo's would surface, reminding me that she had lived here for nearly thirty years before us.

I blew a cobweb off the largest shell, then sneezed. 'I'm going to clean this up and re-thread it,' I decided. 'We can hang it over the baby's cot!' I beamed at him. 'See? I knew cleaning behind the radiator was a good idea! Didn't I tell you?'

As it was Sunday, we were not due to open the café until midday. Ed went to make us both brunch, while I set about untangling each string and taking off the shells. I washed them in warm soapy water and cleaned the driftwood. Then I hunted through my sewing box for some sparkly ribbon to replace the string. It would look so pretty! I loved the idea of making a connection between Jo and the baby, linking the generations in the café.

'You are going to love this, Walnut,' I said to my bump, as I set out the pieces on the coffee table. Through the window of the living room I could see the golden sand of Carrawen Bay and the surfers in action on the tumbling waves. It was a view I never tired of, especially on a sunny July morning like today. 'You can lie in your cot and watch the shells swinging, like a proper beach-baby,' I added. 'How cool is that?'

I felt a squirming inside, as Walnut made a slow watery turn. We had been calling the baby Walnut ever since week eleven of the pregnancy. 'Your baby is now the size of a walnut,' I had read aloud from a website, and the nickname had stuck. It was all very well, but I just couldn't decide on a proper name for him or her. The baby had been 'Walnut' to us for so long that no other names felt quite right.

'What are we going to call you then, little swimmer?' I asked aloud, putting my hands on my belly. At first I had had romantic notions of calling our child after one of our ancestors. But a glance through my family tree was not promising. Not unless I wanted to call the baby Jean, Harold, Edgar, Dorothy or Keith, anyway. Funnily enough, I did not. My sisters had five children between them and they had already used all my favourite names. 'How about Sasha? Emily? Daniel?' I said, trying some other names aloud. 'Arthur? May? Beatrice?'

'Food's ready,' called Ed just then. I waddled through to the kitchen, where we had a small dining table at the far end. I had already eaten a bowl of porridge and two bananas that morning, but I was famished again.

Of course, as a chef, Ed couldn't dish up any old rubbish – he prided himself on making it all look delicious. The bacon was crispy, the sausages were plump. And the toast was buttered slices of the loaf he had made yesterday, golden and crunchy. He had added a glass of orange juice and a Danish pastry, in case I fancied it. (We both knew I would.)

'So,' Ed said, as we both began tucking in, 'we really need to start planning for Walnut's arrival.'

I nodded, my mouth full. There are a *lot* of advantages in being married to a chef, believe me. Great breakfast skills come pretty high on my list. 'Yes,' I replied. 'I should write my birth plan.'

I already had a few ideas for the birth plan. The main one was: make the pain stop. Seriously. I didn't care how. They could knock me out and I would not object. Also on my list: no whale music or pan pipes. No mean comments about my stretch-marks or big maternity underwear. And no photos or video footage of me gurning through the contractions.

'I didn't mean the birth plan,' Ed said, breaking into my thoughts. 'I meant your maternity leave. We need to sort out some cover in the café for when it all kicks off.'

'Oh, right. Yes.' At weekends we were helped out by Josh, a seventeen-year-old from the village. Over the last two summers, we had taken on extra staff members too: local teenagers or students. It would be wise to find people sooner rather than later, I supposed.

'When the baby comes, I can call in an agency chef to cover for me,' Ed said. 'But we should hire a café manager quite soon. That way, you can have some time off before the birth.'

I swallowed a lump of toast impatiently. 'But *I'm* the café manager,' I said. I didn't like the thought of another person taking over. No one else could love the place as much as me, or do half as good a job. Jo had trusted me with the Beach Café when she died. It was down to me to see it through. 'Anyway, I'm right here, on site. I'm sure we can manage.'

One of my sisters, Louise, had sent me a parcel of her children's old baby things the other week, including a sling. I had pictured myself back behind the café counter almost straight away. The baby would be strapped to me, learning the family business from day one. It would be adorable!

'Evie, you'll be tired after the birth,' Ed told me. 'We don't know how long you'll have to stay in hospital. And before then, you should rest anyway. Every time my mum rings, she asks if you're putting your feet up yet.'

I pulled a face. 'Mine, too,' I said. Everyone kept telling me that. *Put your feet up. Just relax. Take it easy. Do nothing!*

I was not very good at sitting still, though. Never had been. Even with my huge belly, swollen ankles and heartburn, I preferred to keep busy. Now that summer was under way, our café was coming into its most hectic period of the year, and there was a lot to do.

There had been two very hot weekends already this month, when we had served a record number of ice creams and sold out of pasties. The school holidays began in three weeks, and then business would be non-stop until

September. I didn't have time to 'take it easy' or 'do nothing'. I had worked really hard over the last two years to make the café a success. Baby or no baby, I was not about to turn my back on the café. I couldn't!

'Well, I'm definitely having a fortnight of paternity leave,' Ed went on. 'I want to make the most of it, spend some proper time off together – our new family. We'll never have those first few weeks again, will we?'

He had a point. And I wanted all that too. Of course I did. When I thought about the brand-new little person inside me, I felt as if I might melt with excitement. I couldn't *wait* to meet our baby – William, Kate, Fred, Ginger – whatever we ended up calling this real human being, who was half-me, half-Ed. We were going to be a family!

I felt confused, though. The baby was still an unknown factor. However excited I was, I could not quite imagine our new life together, three of us rather than two. The café, on the other hand, I knew inside out. And the best way to run it was to have me behind the counter. Why didn't Ed see that?

'Let's see how we get on,' I said in the end.

Maybe if we stopped talking about it, Ed would change his mind. We could manage without anyone else in my beloved café, I told myself. Of course we could!

There was only one tiny thing I had not thought of. Ed might be gorgeous and charming and kind but, like me, he was also stubborn. Once he decided something, there was no stopping him. I should have known better.

It was a cloudless day that Sunday, and we had a steady stream of customers lining up for Ed's famous bacon-and-egg-roll brunches. Josh and I were so busy that it was a while before I could slip out from behind the counter and clear some tables. We had a large decked terrace at the front of the café, which was always the first place to fill up on sunny days. Mindful of the greedy seagulls, I stacked a tray with ketchup-smeared plates and empty coffee cups. Then I wiped down the tables ready for new customers.

I was just making my way back inside when I saw the sign. Stuck up in the front window for all to see was a small white piece of card. In Ed's writing, I read:

WANTED: CAFÉ MANAGER AND TWO ASSISTANTS. IMMEDIATE START.

Chapter Two
Helen

Was it possible to be bored in paradise? Thirty-five-year-old Helen Fraser had been surprised to discover that the answer was yes. She felt bad even admitting it to herself, though. What was wrong with her? She and her husband, Paul, had moved to Cornwall, a mile from the sea. The scenery was stunning. The weather was lovely. They had left behind their stressful city lives for a relaxing break. Lucky you, their friends had all sighed. And yet here she was, feeling the first stirrings of boredom after just a fortnight. She must be the most ungrateful person on earth.

Everyone had been shocked when Helen and Paul announced their decision. For years they had run a successful gastro pub in a leafy Birmingham suburb. They had changed it from a run-down old boozer into a light-filled, classy place to meet friends, with the best pub menu around. It had taken them five years to build up a solid business, and the till never stopped ringing. The long hours and hard grind had taken their toll, though. Living above your own pub meant you could never get away: it took over your whole world. Helen had wanted a different sort of life for some time now. They both had.

'Maybe we need a change,' Helen said back in February, when they had both come down with flu, one after the other. Things had been tough lately. She had been in and out of hospital a few times in the months leading up to Christmas ('Women's problems,' she heard Paul telling a customer, and cringed). They had had a break-in just after New Year. Then there was the awful incident with Leanne Carpenter (Helen was trying not to think about that), followed by the flu. Helen had never felt so poorly. Despite her best efforts to stay healthy, she knew she was run-down. 'I love the pub and all our regulars, but we could do with a break,' she said. 'We can't go on like this forever.'

Paul agreed. He was run-down and tired, too. It had taken him a full three weeks to shake off the illness. They had both worked their entire lives, leaving school at sixteen and going straight into jobs. Enough was enough. And so, that spring, they decided to sell the pub and treat themselves to a grown-up gap year. Why not? Life was short, and it was high time they had some fun. Tempted by the idea of a new life by the seaside, they rented a pretty white-painted cottage in Perracombe, north Cornwall, on a twelve-month contract. 'But what will you *do* all day?' their friends asked. 'Won't you get bored?'

Helen and Paul had laughed at these questions. Running a busy pub seven days a week, they could barely remember what it felt like to be bored. Besides, Helen was looking forward to being in a place where nobody knew her, for a change. There would be no whispering voices, no worried looks. Nobody saying, 'Did you hear what happened with Helen and Leanne? I couldn't believe it! The police came and everything!'

They could escape from all that in Cornwall, thank goodness. Bring on the peace and quiet, thought Helen. It couldn't come soon enough. And please, please let her feel healthy and strong again. Please let this be the right time.

Yet now here they were, living their stress-free new life . . . and it turned out that peace and quiet could be stressful in its own way. Not for Paul, of course. He had palled-up with a couple of blokes in the village pub – he was that sort of person. He had spent the whole of last weekend away on a forty-mile coastal bike ride with his new mates, returning tired but jubilant. When he wasn't on his bike, he would get up at dawn to catch the best waves for surfing, or take himself off fishing all day. It turned out that peace and quiet suited Paul just fine.

'Come with me!' he kept saying. 'Do you good to get out of the house. It's a cracking morning.'

But Helen didn't want to go surfing or fishing, or put herself through mad cycle rides with a load of blokes. She saw him off each time with a smile, but as soon as he left the house, her smile vanished. The truth was that, for the first time in years, she felt lonely. She was not used to being on her own. At the pub she had her regulars for company, and she had known hundreds of people. Here she was nobody. She felt as if she had forgotten how to chat, let alone make a new friend.

Had they done the right thing? She wondered one morning, on her own again in the cottage. Paul had gone surfing, leaving before she was even awake. Helen didn't know what to do with herself. Earlier that week she had pottered about the garden. She had walked to the nearest beach and sketched some of the children playing. She had baked a carrot cake, Paul's favourite. All lovely things to do – all things she had never had time for, back in Birmingham – but she was on her own the whole time. Left alone, she could feel the bad thoughts creeping back in again, circling like vultures.

They had given themselves a year here, a year to unwind and recover from hurts gone by. But what if they still couldn't . . . ?

She stopped before she could finish the question in her own mind. Stop being so negative, she told herself. Forget what happened in the past. Get over it!

Fed up with her own company, Helen jumped up from the sofa. Paul had the right idea. He was out there, enjoying himself. It was time she did the same.

Before she could change her mind, she pushed her feet into her old trainers, grabbed the house keys and her purse and headed out to the small shed where they kept their bikes. Swinging a leg over the saddle, she took off, pedalling with new resolve. She didn't have a clue where she was going, but it was another bright sunny morning, too nice to be stuck indoors with only her dark thoughts for company. She had to do *something*.

*

Helen cycled inland for a while, past farms and through tiny villages, admiring the lush green landscape around her. She breathed in the clean salty air – so different from the smog on the Birmingham Ring Road – and tried to relax. It would be okay, she told herself. This was a different way of life, that was all. She just had to be brave, try and get to know people. She had to 'put herself out there', as Paul said. Above all, she had to remain hopeful. They both badly wanted Cornwall to be the answer to their prayers and wishes. Neither of them had said 'last-chance saloon' out loud, but Helen couldn't help thinking it, in private.

The cycle ride helped a bit. She felt her spirits lift as she headed back towards the coast road. She crested the brow of a hill and saw the sea laid out before her, like a glittering blue cape. It was so pretty here, like something from a painting. They *were* lucky, she thought. This was the real deal.

She cycled on towards the sea, no longer quite sure where she was. Even better! A real adventure, she told herself, her long brown hair streaming behind her in the wind. She coasted down a hill and a sign appeared on the left, telling her she was entering the village of Carrawen Bay. The name rang a bell. She was pretty sure it was only a few miles from Perracombe. She must have cycled in a large circle.

Carrawen Bay was very sweet, on first impressions. There was an old stone schoolhouse, a village hall and a small parade of shops. Then the road gave way to sand dunes and the beach. She braked at the bottom of the hill, her nose twitching at the scent of hot bread from the Carrawen Bakery. Delicious! It was a bit early for lunch, but she was hungry after her cycle ride. She was just chaining her bike to the railings when she spotted a café on the beach itself. Perfect.

Helen followed the path down to the sand. To reach the café, you had to climb up a flight of wide wooden steps which led to an open terrace, full of chairs and tables, with parasols open to provide shade. She was not a fanciful person, but there was a lovely feel to the place, she thought. Families and couples filled the tables, and everyone seemed to be in a cheerful holiday mood. Hardly surprising, she thought, when a good-looking man emerged with a tray of steaming golden pasties and cold drinks.

She was just about to follow him inside when a notice in the front window caught her eye:

17

*WANTED: CAFÉ MANAGER AND TWO
ASSISTANTS. IMMEDIATE START.*

Helen took a sharp intake of breath. Maybe this was a sign. Hadn't she just been thinking that she needed some purpose again, that she missed being around other people? She could do a café manager job standing on her head. It would be easy and fun, and, unlike the pub, she would be able to walk away at the end of a shift and switch off. It might even stop her dwelling on all the things that had gone so wrong, back in Birmingham.

With her mind made up, she squared her shoulders, took a deep breath and went in.

Chapter Three

Evie

Being pregnant was like becoming public property, I had found. Complete strangers seemed to like nothing more than to offer a pregnant woman unwanted advice. *Let me bore on about what you should or shouldn't do, when it's none of my business. Listen while I frighten you with gruesome birth details that you don't want to hear. Wait! Come back! I haven't told you about my stitches yet!*

It wasn't just random strangers, either. My mum and my sisters, Ruth and Louise, had bombarded me with information from day one. Not a week went by without Mum sending me some snippet from the *Daily Telegraph* about scary pregnancy problems, or what not to eat. (For someone who could scoff an entire wheel of Camembert in one sitting, it was never good news.) Ruth texted details of special offers at Baby Gap and Petit Bateau, and gloated about how hard the first few months of no sleep would be. (Sample comment: 'It's *hell*.') And Louise emailed helpful pieces of Buddhist wisdom, videos of useful yoga poses and advice to 'cherish your sex life while you still can' – which didn't exactly fill me with hope.

In the café, it was open season when it came to the personal remarks about my new shape. I had lost count of the customers who had said, 'Aren't you big? Are you sure it's not twins in there?' (Rude.) One woman had shrieked, 'My goodness! The size of your ankles, darling!' as I wiped her table. (She was lucky she didn't get the cloth in her face.)

Other customers had offered a variety of seaside-based names, all the way from Pearl to Shelly to Sandy. And now, in the waiting room of the antenatal clinic, I had made the mistake of chatting to a woman who was on her fourth pregnancy. There was one torn-vagina story that I was very keen to bleach out of my memory.

I had never been so glad to hear my name called for my appointment. I almost broke into a sprint as I left Torn-Vagina Woman mid-sentence and followed Maria, my midwife, into her office.

'So, let me see . . . thirty-five weeks pregnant now,' said Maria, when we were both seated. 'And how are you feeling?'

Err, scared of tearing my lady-parts all of a sudden? 'Excited,' I said instead. 'And exhausted. It's so hard to get to sleep. If I'm not heaving myself off to the loo every two minutes, I'm trying to find a way to roll over that doesn't involve a crane or a pick-up truck.'

Maria smiled. 'There's no easy way to turn over at your stage,' she agreed. 'But some women find it more comfortable sleeping with pillows wedged behind their back and between their legs. Try not to have any drinks after seven o'clock in the evening, too. That might prevent so many loo trips.' She put a blood-pressure cuff around my arm. 'Let's see what's happening here,' she said.

I sat still while the cuff puffed up with air and tightened for a few seconds. Maria took the reading and made a note of the results. 'Hmm,' she said. 'One hundred and forty over ninety. Your blood pressure is rather high. You need to rest more. Have you been overdoing things lately?'

'No,' I said. 'I'm fine. I mean . . .' I thought of how busy we'd been at the café the Saturday

21

before. A sell-out dinner shift had meant that we did not finish until after midnight. 'No more than usual, anyway.'

'You have to start slowing down,' she told me. 'Your body is using an enormous amount of energy right now, as the baby grows. Even while you're sitting here, it's working hard. You have to take things easier, ready for the birth.' She did the usual urine test and looked less stern, thank goodness. 'Well, there's no trace of protein in your pee, which is good news. All the same, I'd like you to come back tomorrow and have the GP take your blood pressure again. Just to be on the safe side.'

'But . . .' I said. Tomorrow was Wednesday and we were expecting a coach full of day-trippers to the beach. We had already planned to run a cream-tea special for them. It would be mayhem if poor Ed was left to run things on his own.

'Evie, this is important. Your blood pressure might be a one-off today, but if your reading is high tomorrow too, we will have to start moni-toring you. We might even have to think about you going into hospital early, or inducing the birth, if it continues. I'm not saying this to alarm you. I just want you to be aware of the risks. You really do have to put the baby first from now on, and listen to your body. All right?'

I felt terrible, then, as if I had somehow let the baby down. As if I had failed a motherhood test before I had even given birth. And I really did not want to go into hospital any earlier than I needed to. 'All right,' I mumbled, one hand on my belly. *Sorry, Walnut. Sorry, Fifi, Zelda, Horatio, Ranulph . . . I'm doing my best. I promise I will try harder, okay?*

I drove home, trying to be serene and relaxed, even when I got distracted at the traffic lights by the sight of a nice red pram, and the driver behind beeped me. Calm thoughts, I reminded myself, and puffed out a long slow breath. From here until the birth, I would glide through life, without any stress. No problem.

The air was soft and summery as I arrived back in Carrawen. The beach was full of happy children, and the few clouds in the sky were small and puffy, like cute little rabbit pillows. There was even a leftover flake of croissant in my cleavage, which still tasted good. (Just joking. Honest.)

I turned off the engine and my fingers went up to the silver Christmas-tree necklace I had been wearing ever since I first found out I was pregnant. It had become a talisman for me, a lucky charm. I had even worn it on our wedding day in May, hidden under a big, sparkly rhinestone-and-pearl choker.

It was all good, I told myself, taking deep breaths. It was all going to be fine.

I walked up the sandy metal steps around the back of the café and unlocked the kitchen door. 'I'm back!' I called cheerfully, just in time to see Ed shaking hands with a thirty-something woman at the café counter. 'See you on Monday,' he said to her as she left.

I went over to him, putting on my apron. 'Who was that?' I asked. Like I hadn't already guessed.

He wheeled around, looking guilty at my question. 'Oh! I didn't hear you come in,' he said. 'That was Helen. Our new manager. She and her husband have just moved down from Birmingham. They've been running their own pub for years, so she should be perfect.'

I sniffed. Perfect? There was only one *perfect* manager for our Beach Café, and that was me. 'A pub is very different to a café,' I said, feeling tetchy. I didn't like the way Ed had gone behind my back to interview her, let alone offer her the job without giving me a say. Was this how it was going to be from now on? Me

24

shunted to the side while he made all the big decisions? The very thought had me bristling.

'It'll be fine,' Ed said. 'She seems great, and she knows it's only short-term. Come on, don't be like that. We talked about it, remember? This way the café stays open while we get to spend proper time with Walnut. It's win-win for everyone.'

The baby moved inside me as I tied the apron strings behind my back. 'You should have let me meet her first,' I said. Ed and I never usually argued, but today my temper was on a knife-edge. 'I might be pregnant, but I haven't lost all my brain cells, you know. I would have liked to judge her for myself. As she's taking my place, and all that!'

He looked a bit startled at how cross I was. 'Sorry – she just seemed too good to turn down,' he said. 'There's nothing sinister about it. She came in, and you weren't here, so I made the decision for both of us.'

I folded my arms across the bump and looked away. I knew I was going over the top, but it all seemed to be happening too quickly. I had always been such a control freak about the café. I hated feeling left out of anything.

'Evie, come on,' Ed said, with a trace of irritation in his voice. 'I'm just thinking of what's best for you, and for this place. Anyway, Helen is great. I'm sure you'll really like her.'

Call me contrary or just pig-headed, but when someone says, 'You'll love this,' I instantly think, 'No, I won't.' And so I set my jaw and said nothing in reply to Ed's comment. We'll see about that, I thought stubbornly.

Chapter Four

Evie

I kept myself calm with more nesting. I painted the spare room a pale blue, the exact colour of the sea first thing in the morning. I assembled the bits of cot that my sister Ruth had given us and put a soft yellow sheet on the mattress. Then I washed the pile of teeny newborn baby clothes and blankets that my sisters and friends had passed on to me. Everyone had been so kind when it came to giving us stuff. 'Ah, that's mothers for you,' my mum said when we chatted on the phone. 'All mums like to pass things on. Whether it's cots or prams or advice, or even just a bit of support. That's what we do. You'll see.'

There was just one job left to make Walnut's bedroom perfect. With a bit of swearing and some cack-handed drilling, I hung the restored shell-mobile from the ceiling. When the sun fell on the gold ribbon, it cast tiny sparkles of light, freckling the pale walls. I opened the window to let in the sea breeze, and the shells clinked and jingled together, just as I remembered.

I felt a rush of nostalgia, as well as pride in my own work. 'That's a mobile fit for a little seaside prince or princess, Walnut. Or George or Charlotte or . . . I don't know, Leia?' I said. 'Whatever your name is, you are going to love it!'

The next day was drizzly and cool: bad news for business, but good news for my poor swollen ankles, which puffed to the size of butternut squash in hot weather. Today they were only avocado-sized which felt skinny in comparison. I went back to the GP with a sense of doom, but my blood pressure seemed to have settled down a little, thank goodness.

'But don't work too hard,' she warned, as I heaved myself up to leave. 'You should be taking things more easily now, okay? Come back next week, so I can keep an eye on you.'

The café was quiet when I returned so I busied myself cleaning behind the coffee machine. With our new manager, Helen, starting the next day, I wanted to have everything looking perfect.

'Excuse me,' came a voice, and I turned to see a fifty-something woman. She had russet-red hair in a shingled bob and was wearing a pink fleece and cut-off jeans. Her eyes flitted to all the corners of the café, and a strange look was on her face. 'You're not . . . ? No, you can't be Jo – you're too young. Is Jo still working here, by any chance?'

'Jo? Oh.' I felt my face cloud. I still missed my lovely aunty. She had been the most fun, spirited person I had ever met. 'I'm sorry to say she died a few years ago,' I replied. Her car had been hit by a lorry, driving too fast down into Carrawen, and she was gone, just like that.

The woman's face fell. 'I'm so sorry,' she said. Then there was an awkward pause for a few seconds. 'Are you . . . ? Is this your café now?' she asked.

'Yes,' I said, hoping I wasn't going to be in any trouble. Mind you, if Environmental Health were about to do a spot-check, they had picked the right time, at least. There wasn't a single speck of dust or dirt to be found in the café after all my scrubbing. Bring on the inspection. 'I'm Evie, Jo's niece. Can I help you?'

She gave a strange smile, and her eyes swung around the room again. 'I haven't been here for years,' she said slowly. Her voice had a Welsh lilt, I noticed. 'We moved away when I was ten.' She stuck a hand out. 'I'm Morwenna. I was actually born upstairs in the flat. My dad built this place, back in his day. Wouldn't recognise it now, mind!'

I gaped with delight. 'Your dad *built* the café? How wonderful!' Jo had run the café for so many years that I had never really thought about anyone living here before her. 'When was that? And why did you leave?' I remembered my manners. 'Oh – can I get you a drink? I'd love to chat, if you can spare the time.'

'Of course,' she said. 'I'd love that too. I can't quite believe I'm here!'

Morwenna and I sat in the corner booth while she talked through her memories. Her dad had built the café way back when, and he and his wife had run the place for fifteen years. In the meantime, Morwenna and her brother, Gerren, – good Cornish names, she told me – were born right here under the café roof. 'Mum had a thing about hospitals,' she said. 'Decided she would rather have us at home, up in the flat.'

I couldn't stop smiling. I loved the fact that Morwenna had walked in out of the blue and was able to fill in so much of the café's history for me. She and her brother had helped behind the counter from an early age, she said, just as I planned for Walnut to do in the future. They had moved to Wales when she was about ten, when her mum's parents became ill and needed looking after. 'Mum and Dad were heartbroken to leave,' she said. 'But Dad knew the place would be in good hands, once he met Jo.'

'And did they come back to visit at all? Did you return for family holidays here?'

Morwenna shook her head. 'We never did,' she said. 'Dad was a Cornish man through and through. I think he was worried it would make him too sad. Moving to Wales was meant to be short-term but then Gerren and I settled into our new schools, and my parents started a bed-and-breakfast business. We were happy there. After a while Cornwall felt like a long way away.' She gave me a crooked smile, but her eyes were sad. 'It's lovely to be back.'

I wanted to hug her, but managed to stop myself just in time. My pregnancy boobs were so massive that I was in danger of smothering innocent victims with a single cuddle. 'And it's lovely to have you,' I said instead. 'You and your family are welcome any time. Cream teas whenever you want – on the house, okay?'

*

Meeting Morwenna really made my day. Sadly, her parents had long since passed away, but she promised to give my best wishes to Gerren. She also said she would make a point of coming back another time to see the newest addition to the Beach Café family. 'It's the best place in the world to grow up,' she told me as we said good-bye. 'Lucky baby! He or she will have such a wonderful childhood.'

Her words stayed with me for the rest of the afternoon. A lucky baby? I really hoped so. I wasn't sure that I was going to be the greatest mum ever, in all honesty. I had been tired and grumpy lately, and I had a hot temper and a lack of patience. Deep down, I worried that I wasn't even grown-up enough to be a very good parent. My sisters had already told me – kind of smugly – that I should forget all about sleeping and lie-ins and a social life, for the next ten years or so.

'I spent *days* forgetting to brush my own teeth,' Ruth had warned.

'I was feeding Matilda one day when the doorbell rang,' Louise had said airily, 'and I opened the door to the postman with my boob hanging out.'

As my sisters were both more grown-up and together than I had ever been, I couldn't help but find this scary. Life as I knew it seemed to be trickling to a close. From tomorrow the new café manager would move into my place behind the counter, while I was forced to take a back seat. Then, when the baby arrived, I'd find myself in a whole new world – a world where teeth went unbrushed, and casual flashing at the postman was not unusual. Somehow I'd have to learn how to care for our child, to feed and wash and soothe this tiny new person. What if I couldn't do it? What if I was a failure?

It's the best place in the world to grow up, Morwenna repeated in my head. But the worries refused to budge. Having a baby felt like diving into unknown waters. I just had to hope I could stay afloat.

Chapter Five
Helen

'You've done what?' Paul said when Helen cycled home and told him she had got a job. 'Why, though? We're meant to be on holiday, remember. Relaxing!'

'I know, but . . .' She shrugged. 'It's something to do – that's all.'

They were sitting in the back garden, having a barbecue. It still felt novel, having evenings to themselves, not to mention their own private garden. Of course there had been a beer garden at the pub, with wooden tables set out for punters in the summer months. But Helen and Paul were always too busy serving their customers to sit out there themselves.

'I don't get it,' he said, turning the steaks with the tongs. The meat sizzled and spat. 'I thought we had come here to chill out, not get jobs. Waitressing in a café! I mean . . . What's that all about?'

'I just felt lonely,' Helen confessed. 'There's plenty for you to do here. You're out every day. I didn't know what to do with myself.'

Paul shook his head. 'But Helen, I thought we wanted the same thing? I thought we came to Cornwall so that we could get away from all the stress and . . .' He didn't finish the sentence, but he didn't need to. 'You know.'

'Yes. And I want that, too. You know I do. Look, it's not going to be for long. The guy I spoke to – Ed – he was quite vague. His wife's not well, or something. He said she was going to be out of action for a couple of months, so . . .'

'What's wrong with her?'

'I'm not sure. He seemed a bit distracted.' It had been a very quick interview, because the man seemed to be running the place on his own. Helen tried to remember the words he had used as they stood behind the counter chatting. *Evie – my wife – will be off for a while. She's at the doctor's now, which is why I'm on my own at the moment. Oh, hello there, can I help you? Excuse me a minute, Helen.*

Poor woman. 'Off for a while' – that sounded serious. No wonder Ed hadn't wanted to go into details. Helen had seen her fair share of doctors, too. *We can't find any medical reason for the mis-carriages*, the last doctor had said, her eyes kind behind little gold-rimmed glasses. She had patted Helen awkwardly as she lay in the hospital bed, passing her a tissue when she couldn't stop crying.

Paul still looked miffed, Helen noticed, as her thoughts came back to the present. 'You should have said you felt lonely,' he told her. 'You said you liked pottering about on your own. I thought you were happy!'

'I *am* happy,' she said, although even she could hear the lack of conviction in her voice. 'And the café closes at five most afternoons. We'll still have nearly every evening together.'

He prodded the steaks again and didn't reply immediately.

'Sorry,' she said after a moment. 'I should have run it past you. I'm not doing very well at this seaside lifestyle, am I? With a bit of luck, once I've got to know a few people, I'll be fine. And it's a gorgeous little café. Gives me something to do. You know me – I like feeling useful.'

'I know,' he said. 'You just took me by surprise, that's all. But if that's what you want to do . . .'

She nodded. 'I think it is,' she said. 'I'll give it a go anyway.'

*

It was a beautiful cycle ride between Perracombe and Carrawen Bay, and Helen enjoyed her first commute to the café very much. This was more like it! No traffic jams. No stress. A bit of exercise, beach views, human contact . . . It was exactly what she needed. She walked into the café five minutes early for her first shift, only to stop dead in her tracks.

There, behind the counter, was a heavily pregnant woman with dark curly hair and an apron. Someone had written in red marker pen on the front of the apron, 'NO! IT'S NOT TWINS!'

Helen's heart gave a painful thump. *Oh, no,* she thought.

Her breath felt tight in her lungs. Maybe she should turn and walk straight out again? Jobs were easy come, easy go in the café industry, just like in the pub world. Nobody would care if she bailed out, surely? In a nice place like this, the job would be snapped up by someone else in a day or two. She was on the verge of an abrupt about-turn when the pregnant woman looked up and noticed her. 'Oh! Hello. I don't suppose you're Helen, are you?' she called.

Busted! 'Yes,' Helen said and stepped forward reluctantly. So that was what the chef-guy had meant about his wife being out of action. Not ill at all. Just pregnant. Typical of Helen's luck! She never would have applied for the job if she had known. Nobody liked having their nose rubbed in it.

'Nice to meet you,' said the woman, although her smile seemed kind of fake, as if she didn't mean a word of it. 'I'm Evie. Let me get you an apron and I'll show you around.'

She was drinking coffee, Helen noticed in disapproval. Everyone knew that pregnant women were meant to avoid coffee! It was like Leanne Carpenter all over again, she thought with a lurch of dread. And, goodness knows, she had already been there, done that, had the little chat with the stern-faced policeman . . .

She shook the memory away before it could sink its claws in. *Don't think about Leanne Carpenter. That's in the past. Over.*

She put on the apron and tried to listen while the woman – Evie – showed her how to work the coffee machine. *Come on, Helen. You can do this. Get a grip. Move on.*

But it was so *unfair*, she thought in the next moment, as grief and heartache burst up inside her. And it hurt so much! When would the pain be over?

Chapter Six
Evie

A week passed in the café and our mighty staff of two, plus Josh at weekends, swelled to an even mightier five. Josh finished his exams and began working four days a week, plus Friday and Saturday evenings. Aged seventeen, he was tall, sporty and handsome, and brought in droves of extra giggling female teenagers. (Good for business.)

Then we had Tilly, a year younger, red-haired and freckled, who sang along with the radio in a sweet, high voice. She had just done her GCSEs and was willing to work all the shifts we could give her. (Excellent.)

And then there was Helen, the perfect new café manager, according to Ed. Thirty-something Helen, with the smooth brown ponytail and trim figure, so different from my great bulk. Perfect Helen, who never quite looked me in the eye, and who froze me out when I tried to speak to her. I didn't get it. I just did not understand.

I had always prided myself on being one of those people who could get along with anyone. I loved chatting away to customers and staff, passing the time of day with a gossip if business was slow. Shy? Not me. At a loss for words? Never. But Helen didn't play ball. Right from the first morning, she seemed to take against me, and I had no idea why.

With customers, she was friendly and professional. She could spot a spilled drink or a dropped scone across the room, and always acted at once, rather than waiting for someone else to notice. With the rest of the staff, she seemed perfectly nice, too. One morning I walked in to find her hugging Tilly, who had been dumped by her boyfriend the night before and was pink-eyed and tearful. She cheered Josh up when he failed his driving test, and had him laughing minutes later with tales of her dreadful parking.

With me, though, her face closed up like a clam. Ed kept saying I was imagining it, but I knew Helen didn't like me. In fact, there were times when I swear she was trying to wind me up. Like when I overheard her telling Ed that we should buy our cakes from a wholesaler, instead of freshly made from our friend Annie. 'You would save a fortune,' she told him. 'You can definitely get them cheaper.'

My hackles rose, and I found myself having to go and scrub some tables outside, very hard, to calm down. Why did we buy our cakes from Annie? Because she was an ace baker who made everything from scratch in her own kitchen. And also, most importantly, because she was our *friend*. Did that count for nothing in Helen's world?

'Maybe we should order in some metal teapots instead of china ones,' she said to Ed another time, when Josh dropped a tray of crockery. 'They're lighter and don't break so easily. We used them in the pub and found them much more economical.'

'I don't like metal teapots,' I said pointedly, even though Helen had gone into the kitchen to speak to Ed in private. 'They don't pour as well, and children can burn their fingers on them.' *And by the way,* I wanted to add, *hello, I work here too, remember. Even though I'm preggers, I can still have an opinion on a teapot, thank you very much.*

Helen put her hands up and shrugged – *all right, keep your hair on, love* – then glanced at Ed. 'Just trying to be helpful,' she murmured.

My fingers closed so tightly around the Christmas-tree charm on my necklace that I almost expected it to melt. I took a deep breath in an attempt to stay calm. Inside, however, I was finding it very difficult not to flick a V-sign at Helen. Trying to be helpful, indeed. Trying to tip a pregnant woman over the edge, more like. In *my* café!

Worst of all was the time that I came back from an antenatal clinic to find that Helen had taken it upon herself to move all the tables and chairs around. 'We can seat more customers this way,' she said, when she saw my jaw drop. 'Ed thought it was a good idea too, so . . .'

Oh, did he now? I thought crossly. The traitor. The most annoying thing was that Helen was right, much as I hated to admit it. I could tell she was used to running the show, just as I was. We both had set ideas about best practice. And while I probably should have been a bit more grateful that she was trying to make things better for the business, it still rankled.

'It's so unimportant,' Ed said when I moaned to him about it later on. 'It's just chairs and tables, Evie. Chairs and tables. Who cares?'

'But . . .'

'It doesn't matter,' he said. 'Let it go. Please stop getting worked up about stupid things.

Aren't you meant to be watching your blood pressure, anyway? Come on, let's go for a swim and forget about it.'

I bit back my grumbles and pulled on my maternity swimming costume. I might look like a barrage balloon these days, but I still loved a post-work dip in the sea. The weightless feeling of being gently rocked by the waves never failed to boost my mood.

Today we strode through the shallows and I let the cool, clear water pick me up. Ed had already broken into a fast crawl, his muscular tanned arms slicing through the water – one, two, one, two. I did my usual sedate granny breaststroke, feeling a new energy in my tired legs as the sun cast its golden sparkles around me. The water circled around my throat and the Christmas-tree charm floated and bobbed like a tiny silver fish whenever I slowed to a halt.

But the relief of being in the sea and larking about with Ed was not enough to change my mind about Helen. Even when Ed and I had a bit of a smooch and a cuddle, and I said sorry for being so neurotic. Secretly I was crossing my fingers behind my back anyway, because the café layout – and who decided it – *did* matter. Stressing out about such a thing *wasn't* stupid.

Ed didn't understand, that was all. He couldn't see that Helen was trying to push me out of my own space. What was her problem?

Chapter Seven

Helen

It was almost the end of Helen's first week in her new job. The 'Closed' sign hung in the door, Josh and Tilly had gone home and she was cashing up the day's takings. Helen liked the way the café wound down of its own accord around five o'clock. The families would start packing up and herding their sandy children homewards. The beach would slowly empty, the sea magically clearing every last sandcastle and moat. Before long the crowds were but a distant memory and Helen could cycle home to Paul, with lots to tell him about her day.

The door opened just then and a man shuffled in. He was grizzled and weather-beaten, with a light coating of grime, and clutched a handful of bulging carrier bags. Homeless, Helen guessed, as she noticed the filthy trainers on his feet.

'Evening, love. Don't suppose you could spare us a cup of tea, could you?' he asked.

'Sorry, no,' Helen said politely. 'We're closed.' She was aware of the open till drawer and pushed it shut as he came up to the counter. You could never be too careful.

The man's face sagged. 'Oh,' he said. His gaze fell on the cakes still under their glass domes on the counter, and Helen felt a twinge of annoyance. Tilly was meant to have put them into tins before she clocked off. 'Any chance I could have a bit of cake then? If it's going spare?'

Helen folded her arms. 'It's not going spare. Sorry. It's all accounted for and . . .'

Evie, who had been in the stockroom, came back in at that moment and interrupted. 'Of course you can have some cake, Fred. No problem.'

She cast a scathing glance at Helen. 'Would you rather he starved?' Helen's face flamed, as Evie went ahead and cut a wedge of chocolate cake and wrapped it in a paper napkin. 'Here. And did you want a cuppa, too? Coming up.'

'Thanks, love,' said the man, biting hungrily into the cake as soon as Evie gave it to him.

'Well, pardon me for thinking about the business,' Helen said tightly, feeling as if she had been told off by a teacher. Sarcasm burst out of her. 'How stupid of me to worry about your profits!'

Ed appeared from the kitchen. 'What's going on?' he asked, looking from one woman to the other.

Evie ignored him. 'The day I care more about my profits than a man who's down on his luck is the day I quit,' she told Helen. 'There you are, Fred,' she added, handing over a takeaway cup. 'Nice to see you again.'

Helen's hands trembled. She hated the way Evie was always trying to overrule her and keep her in her place. 'Do you want me to be the manager or not?' she blurted out. 'Only I can't carry on like this.'

'Of course we want you to be the manager!' Ed said, taken aback.

Helen ripped off her apron. 'Then have a word with your wife, will you?' she said, before she could stop herself. 'Because she's doing my head in!'

Helen stormed out of the café and began cycling home. After a few miles of hard pedalling, her anger gave way to despair. Once again she had lost her temper and been unable to control herself. *Maybe it's just me,* she thought miserably, as the wind tugged at her hair. *Maybe I'm the sort of person who invites conflict. Maybe I don't deserve a child in the first place.*

There was a lump in her throat and she hunched over the handlebars, feeling half-tempted to cycle straight off the cliff. Would she even have a job, by the time she was back in Perracombe? Evie aside, she really enjoyed working in the Beach Café. She liked Ed, she liked Josh and Tilly, she liked the customers and the beautiful setting. Why couldn't she have kept her mouth shut?

Her phone was ringing in her pocket and she braked to see who it was. 'Ed', she read on the screen. *Oh, God.* He was probably going to sack her, Helen thought with a grimace. Still, she wasn't a coward. She would face the music, she decided, and answered the call. 'Hello?'

'Hi, it's Ed. Listen . . . Sorry about earlier. Evie has been under a lot of pressure recently. But we both want you to stay at the café. I really hope you'll come back tomorrow.'

Helen took a deep breath. 'I'm sorry, too,' she mumbled. 'I was only trying to do what was best for the business, that's all.'

'I know you were – and I appreciate that. We both do.'

Helen didn't reply. She wasn't sure she believed that Evie appreciated anything she had done at the café.

'So . . . are we still colleagues?' Ed asked. A

pleading note entered his voice. 'Do you still want the job?'

Helen hesitated. One more chance, she decided. 'Yes,' she replied. 'We're still colleagues.' Any day now Evie was sure to start her maternity leave, she figured. It could not come soon enough.

Helen cycled the rest of the way home. She replayed in her mind the earlier bust-up and felt angry all over again. Mind you, that was hardly unusual. Working alongside Evie had been non-stop irritation so far. Helen felt prickles of annoyance when Evie moaned about her back aching, or sighed about her heartburn, or customers commented on her size and her eyes went a bit flinty and cross. *Get a grip!* Helen wanted to shout. *Count yourself lucky!* The three times Helen had been pregnant, she had not complained, not once. Not even when she threw up twice a day for four long weeks. She had been so happy. So excited. So keen to do everything properly.

Three miscarriages later, she couldn't help resenting other women who seemed to find the whole process so easy. Women who got pregnant by accident, women who weren't sure they even wanted a baby in the first place.

Helen had overheard Evie laughing with an elderly lady called Florence – a café regular – about how her mother-in-law had been the first one to guess that Evie was pregnant. 'I didn't have a clue,' Evie had said gaily. 'Talk about hopeless!'

Helen had been mopping up a spilled glass of lemonade at the time and had gripped the mop handle so hard she was surprised it didn't snap in two. It was just so unfair. The more she heard about Evie, the more she seemed the sort of person who shambled through life without any kind of plan – yet ended up with everything she could possibly want. Meanwhile there was Helen, who knew exactly what she wanted, but kept having it thrown back in her face.

'I'm not so sure this job was a good idea,' she said glumly to Paul over dinner that evening. They were eating outside in their little garden, but even a large plate of juicy garlic chicken hadn't lifted her spirits. 'I keep thinking about Leanne. I'm worried the same thing will happen again.'

Paul put his arm around her. 'No,' he said. 'It won't. You were under a lot of stress back then. Things just . . . spiralled. But it's different here.'

Helen fell silent, wondering if things really

would be all that different. They had moved to Cornwall, hoping that an easier life would lead to the baby they both longed for. But here she was, still obsessing like before. And she had gone and started her period that morning, too. So that was two weeks of hope down the drain, along with yet another chance.

'Don't worry,' Paul said, as if reading her mind. 'It'll happen. And if it doesn't . . . then we've still got each other. Right? It's your day off tomorrow, so let's plan something really fun, just the two of us.'

Still she said nothing. He was being kind, but sometimes it was so hard to drag herself out of these black moods.

'Come on, Helen,' he said after a moment. 'We'll be all right. I promise.' He had finished his dinner and got to his feet. 'Why don't we go along to the pub? There's a band playing tonight, and they're meant to be good. We can have a drink and a dance. I'll introduce you to a few people.'

He pulled her hand and Helen forced a smile. *We'll be all right.* It had been their motto for the last three years, through each month's cycle of hope, then sadness. Now that she was thirty-five, she knew all too well that the chances of getting pregnant were slipping away like an outgoing tide. *We'll be all right,* they kept saying time and again. But what if they weren't?

In hindsight, Helen shouldn't have been working at all, the night things kicked off with Leanne. As soon as they got back from hospital, she should have gone straight up to bed with a hot-water bottle and a box of chocolates. The doctors had told her as much. Paul said so as well. But she insisted that she would rather keep busy, and that she was sick of lying around in bed feeling sorry for herself. Paul, recognising the stern jut of her jaw, gave in. If she really wanted to work behind the bar, then fine.

Big mistake, Helen. Big, dumb mistake. Trying to tough things out after the doctors had told her it was third time unlucky, and she had lost that baby, too . . . She was an idiot for thinking she could carry on as if nothing had happened.

Leanne Carpenter, the local big-mouth, had come into the pub about half an hour after Helen had begun her shift. Across the room Leanne teetered, swerving in a zigzag, bumping into people as she went. Then she parked herself at the bar and ordered a large vodka tonic, slurring every word in the process.

It was the worst possible situation for Helen

right then. Leanne Carpenter was heavily pregnant with her fourth child – and steaming drunk as well. Helen had seen her locally with her children now and then, and she didn't think Leanne was in any danger of winning a Mother of the Year award. She had noticed Leanne smacking her little boys in the Spar shop, when they tipped over a box of Freddos. Leanne smoked like a chimney too, without a care for the baby in the pram. And now here she was in Helen's pub, ordering a double vodka, when by the look of things she had already drunk plenty. *Not in my pub, you don't,* thought Helen, feeling a rush of anger. *Not today, lady.*

'I'm not going to serve you that,' she said primly. 'You shouldn't be drinking, in your condition.'

Leanne scowled. 'Who the hell are you to tell me what I can and can't do?' she said. 'It's up to me what I drink, and I'd like a large vodka tonic. *Please.*'

Helen felt volcanic with rage. How dare this woman be so careless about her unborn baby? How dare she treat it with such casual disdain, when she herself was desperate to hold on to a baby for longer than fifteen weeks? Helen would have done anything to be in Leanne's position then. Anything at all. In the meantime, she was not going to serve Leanne any alcohol – and that was that.

'You can't have one,' Helen snapped, her voice trembling. 'And I'd like you to leave.'

'Leave? Why? What have I done? I'm not going anywhere, love.'

'Yes, you are. I've asked you to leave, so you're leaving.' Helen came out from behind the bar. Small and slender, she was about half the size of Leanne Carpenter, but was so fired up with fury that she didn't have any fear. She put her hand on Leanne's shoulder, but Leanne pushed her away.

'Oi, get off me! That's assault, that is. Man-handling a pregnant woman!'

'I did not . . .'

'Shoving me around. Getting in my face. What's your problem? I've a good mind to call the police about this.'

'What's going on?' And there was Paul, just up from the cellar, looking startled to see his wife involved in a spat. 'What's the problem?'

'Your missus – that's the problem,' Leanne said angrily. She got down from the bar stool and pushed Helen away. 'That's the last time I come in this shit-hole!'

Helen's breath was knocked out of her as she

stumbled backwards, clutching at the bar to keep her balance. 'Good!' she spluttered as Leanne staggered towards the door. 'Because you are not welcome, do you hear me?'

The pub fell silent as everyone stared. With her face hot, Helen pushed her way back through the bar and up to their flat, where she burst into floods of tears.

That wasn't even the worst of it. An hour later the police were round, saying they had been called about an assault on one of the customers. Could Mrs Helen Fraser please answer a few questions?

Thankfully there were enough witnesses to back up Helen's side of the story. She had not assaulted Leanne Carpenter. She had perhaps been a bit shrill and critical, but she had not caused any kind of criminal offence. All the same, word got out. The story became wilder as it travelled. People began giving Helen odd looks, as if they really believed that she and Leanne had had a fist-fight, scrapping on the pub floor like school kids.

Ever since then, Helen had tried to keep herself away from pregnant women. It was just easier that way.

Chapter Eight

Evie

By the end of July I was roughly the size of Wales, with knockers like twin airships and a belly that entered the room several minutes before the rest of me caught up. My stretch-marks were so awful they could probably be tracked by NASA. As if that wasn't enough, the pregnancy hormones had turned my hair into an oil slick, and I became more short-tempered by the day. I felt a bit guilty for pulling rank with Helen over the incident with Fred, but I was sick of her trying to take over. Besides, I had never been one to turn away someone in need. 'Sorry about last night,' I had muttered the next time Helen came into work, but she merely pursed her lips and glared as if she hated me. So that was that.

Then, after another high blood-pressure rating, my midwife, Maria, laid down the law. *Enough,* she told me. I had to stop working now or put the baby at risk. And so, with these words of doom in my ears, I hung up my apron and began my maternity leave. Handing over control of my café was not easy, I can tell you. I had never been a jealous type of person, but I couldn't help feel a pang whenever I heard Helen's laugh floating up the stairs to the flat and I thought about her and Ed running the place together. Without me.

I was probably over-reacting, I told myself. No, I was almost certainly over-reacting. Not only had the hormones left my hair a disaster area, but they were ramping up all my emotions to the level of Extremely Sensitive.

I sobbed over a local news story about a brave dog that helped to rescue his pensioner owner after he fell into a river. I burst into tears of gratitude when my friend Annie gave me a patchwork blanket that she had made for the baby. I found myself dwelling far too much on how pretty Helen was compared to me. And on how Ed seemed to have a new spring in his step, now that he was going off to work with Helen every morning.

I couldn't help remembering how the two of us had fallen in love down in the café during that first heady summer together. What if history went and repeated itself in the worst possible way?

*

When the café closed up that first night and I heard Helen, Tilly and Josh all calling goodbye, I went downstairs. Secretly I was hoping the place would be a tip, and that it had been all too much for Helen and the others to cope with, now that I wasn't there. I'm ashamed to say I even felt a tiny bit disappointed when I saw that the café area was sparkling clean, the floor freshly mopped. Everything was in its place, with not a stray crumb to be seen.

Any normal person would have been pleased that such good care was being taken of their business. Me? I felt more than ever as if I had been put out to pasture, as if I was no longer needed around there.

'Hey,' said Ed, strolling through from the kitchen just then. 'How was your first day of maternity leave?'

'Quiet,' I replied. I had been for a swim and then lumbered into the village to see Annie for tea and cake. I had read the latest 'inspiring' texts from my sister Louise, and had packed up my hospital bag. And then I had had a two-hour nap on the sofa. I was pretty sure even a raging bull would have low blood pressure, after a day like that.

It was a warm evening, the sun turning coppery, and the clouds streaked with gold and pink. I put on my flip-flops and we wandered to the sea for a walk – or, rather, a breathless waddle, in my case. The beach was slowly emptying, as parents brushed sand off reluctant children and deflated brightly coloured lilos. Seagulls lingered hopefully, a safe distance away, their beady eyes on sandwich crusts and fallen chips.

I kicked off my flip-flops and paddled in the shallows at the sea's edge, enjoying how the wet sand squidged between my toes. 'This is nice,' I said, feeling the tension ease. I let out a long, raggedy breath and then reached for Ed's hand. 'Sorry if I've been sort of uptight lately.'

He squeezed my fingers. 'Sort of uptight? I hadn't noticed,' he said. This was such a terrible lie that we both started laughing. 'Two weeks to go, eh? I can't wait. It feels a bit like one long Christmas Eve, doesn't it, all the waiting and wondering?'

'If only Father Christmas could just deliver the baby in a nice stocking at the end of the bed, so I didn't have to go through labour,' I said, only half-joking. I had avoided thinking too much about how the baby was actually going to get out of me. My mum had already warned that I would likely be in for a long labour – 'First ones are always slow. I was thirty-six hours with your sisters!' – which did not make me feel any better. Thirty-six hours was like a whole day-and-a-half of pain. How could anyone bear it?

'You'll be fine,' he told me. 'Nothing to it, I reckon. It can't be worse than man-flu, anyway.'

I swiped at Ed, but he dodged away, laughing. 'How did it go with Helen today then?' I asked, trying – and failing – to keep the edge out of my voice. Yes, I was jealous. And yes, it *was* completely pathetic.

'Yeah, good,' he said. Then he caught sight of my face, and the way my lip was sliding out crossly. 'I mean – terrible,' he said, as he caught on. 'Verging on disastrous for most of the day. Just not the same without you.'

'Right,' I said glumly.

He put an arm around me and hugged me. 'Come on. Don't be like that. I know it's weird, but . . .'

'But she is quite attractive,' I mumbled. 'Whereas I am . . . ' I waved my hand in front of my vast watermelon belly, thick ankles and puffy, worried face. 'Not.'

'Oh, Evie, stop! Stop right there.' He swung me round – not an easy feat without haulage equipment – and put his hands on my shoulders. 'Look at me, you crazy hormonal woman, you.

Helen works for us. She's just doing a job for a short space of time, so that you can rest and look after our child. That's all there is to it. Okay? And everything will go back to normal in the end. I promise.'

'Okay,' I said to Ed, biting my lip. 'Sorry. Again. Your wife is an idiot. Sorry to you too, Walnut,' I added, for the benefit of my bump. 'Or Andy, Laura, Novak, Martina, Roger.'

'Engelbert,' Ed added, unhelpfully.

'Germaine, Simone, Maya, Oprah . . .' I tried.

'Harry, Ron, Hermione,' he mused. 'Maybe not Voldemort.'

'Good call,' I said, and sighed. 'It's a nightmare. How are we ever going to decide?'

'The right name will come to us,' he said. 'Jim-Bob?'

I smiled, feeling much better as we started walking again. 'By the way,' I went on. 'Latest advice update from Louise. We're to go out every night before the baby comes, she says. Have dinner, go to the pub, go to the cinema and have lots of wild sex.'

'What, all at once?' he asked, raising an eyebrow in a very suggestive manner. 'That could be arranged. The question is: which first?'

He slid his arm around my waist – or what was left of it – and began kissing my neck in a soft, seductive sort of way. 'There's only one answer in my mind,' I said, glancing over towards the high street. The shutters were being rolled up at Frying Tonight and I could almost smell the salt and vinegar. All of a sudden I was starving again. 'Haddock and chips,' I said. 'And mushy peas. What do you reckon?'

Chapter Nine

Evie

There was just a week to go now before my due date and I had already felt a few contractions, where my belly became so hard it took my breath away. 'They're called Braxton Hicks contractions,' my midwife, Maria, said when I phoned in a panic the first time. 'It's perfectly normal. Just your body having a practice, that's all.'

I raised my eyebrows, astonished that anyone would feel the need to practise extreme pain. 'Err . . . right. Does that mean Walnut – I mean, the baby – will be here soon?'

'It means your body is getting ready for the birth. You could still be waiting a good few weeks yet, though. First babies are often late.'

A few days passed and then it was Saturday. I was starting to lose track of time, now that I no longer had a regular routine. Saturday was 'Change-Over Day', though – the day lots of people left Carrawen Bay at the end of their holidays, swiftly followed by a huge influx of new arrivals in their place. A quietness fell on the village after ten o'clock in the morning, as most people had to be out of their holiday cottages by then. Across Carrawen, beds would be remade and carpets hoovered in the guest houses, while here in the café we would write menus, check stock and plan for the next busy week ahead.

On Saturday afternoon lots of customers would pour in, and the café always became very busy. We also ran a popular evening dinner service on Friday and Saturday nights, which booked up very quickly.

Saturday, in other words, was about the worst day of the week that Walnut could pick to be born. And so, when I felt a few strange twinges around midday on this Saturday, I chose to ignore them. Probably just more Braxton Hicks contractions, I told myself. Yet another practice session before the big day. There was no way I was going to get Ed flapping, when he had so much to do already, not least with a fully booked restaurant that evening. 'Just hang on until tomorrow, will you, Walnut?' I said, typing up the menu for that evening.

In reply came that strange gripping, squeezing sensation again and my attempt to type 'Cornish ale-battered haddock' became *Ccornnnishaaaa*, before my hands fell off the keyboard.

'Right,' I said, taking a few deep breaths. 'Like that, is it? Hmm.'

I busied myself typing the menus and printing them off, then began ironing the tablecloths and napkins for that evening. Friday and Saturday nights were the only times we dressed up the café in restaurant finery – tablecloths and nice cutlery and tealights on the tables. We allowed dinner guests to bring their own alcohol and served a simple menu, and there was always a lively, relaxed air.

It made me feel really proud, seeing the place full of so many people enjoying their evening, especially when the Carrawen locals came to dine here. Tonight, for instance, I knew that Ruby Woodward's family had booked a table for ten to celebrate her eighteenth birthday. Betty from the grocer's shop was having her anniversary dinner with us, too. It felt like a stamp of approval from the village, confirming that we belonged.

I took the tablecloths, napkins and menus downstairs just as Helen was arriving to start her shift. 'Hi,' we said to each other politely, but she bustled into the tiny cloakroom before I could say anything else. Still like that, then. Whatever.

I was just putting everything in the kitchen when I felt another contraction and froze stock-still for a second, clutching the worktop. Ed glanced over at me. 'Everything all right?'

I breathed out in relief as the feeling faded. 'Fine,' I said.

He was peeling a mountain of potatoes and had his frowny face on. It was not the right time to tell him I was having a few contractions, I thought. Anyway, it was almost certainly a false alarm. There was still a whole week before I was due, after all. And hadn't Maria said just the other day that first babies tended to be late?

I was not exactly known for my own time-keeping skills, it had to be said. If the baby was anything like me, he or she was sure to rock up way later than planned. Its first words would be, 'Sorry I'm late! You wouldn't *believe* what happened!' I could be a whole month away from any childbirth action, if the baby chose.

As the afternoon wore on, though, the 'practice' contractions showed no sign of letting up. Either this was a really intense boot-camp-style practice session or something major was actually starting to happen inside me. I paced around the flat, trying to stay calm. It was four-thirty now and the contractions were coming regularly, every fifteen or twenty minutes. Maria had told me not to bother going to the hospital or calling her until they came much closer together – more like five minutes apart.

'We'll just ride it out together,' I said to Walnut (Jacob / Mia / Nathan) as I paced. 'There's no hurry, right? If you could hold out until at least eleven tonight, when dinner is over, that would be great. Please.'

I sucked in a breath and held tight to my silver Christmas-tree charm as another contraction rolled through me. It wasn't painful yet – more a heavy dragging feeling, but it made me fear for what was to come. Sweat trickled between my shoulder blades and I opened all the windows of the flat, gulping in fresh air.

Perhaps Walnut was in a hurry to get going, after all. Perhaps he or she would be an impatient sort of person, fidgety and restless, who couldn't bear to hang around. Perhaps this was just the start of our child surprising me and Ed at every turn. *So, you thought I would be late, did you? Wrong! Here I come, ready or not!*

At last I cracked and phoned my mum. 'You know the first time you went into labour,' I began.

I heard a great gasp of excitement down the line. 'Oh! Has it started, love? Is this it?'

'I think so,' I said in a small voice. I was scared, now that I had got to this point. Scared and excited and aware of just how life-changing the hours to come would be. Mostly scared, though. Trying not to worry about anything tearing. 'My waters haven't broken, but I think I'm having contractions.'

I heard doubt creep into her voice. 'Ahh. You *think* they're contractions? Sounds like you're a way off yet then,' she told me. 'I would sit tight for a bit longer, darling. Walk around. Have a nice bath. Keep calm and wait it out. Once the proper contractions start, you'll know about it.'

Chapter Ten
Evie

The pain came and went. At around six o'clock the contractions seemed to stop and I fell onto the sofa, worn out. *False alarm*, I told myself, shutting my eyes. Have a breather, Walnut (Raphael / Leonardo / Frida / Tracey). Let's do this some other time, yeah?

Forty minutes or so later I felt the now-familiar clenching sensation stronger than ever. We were back in business. I slid from the sofa and knelt on the floor, my chest and head resting on the coffee table, bum sticking up in the air. I must have looked very odd, but somehow it made me feel better. I tried to think back to what my yoga teacher had said – something about breathing through the pain. Yeah, like that would make any difference, I thought darkly, huffing and puffing and noticing a strange sort of growling noise under my breath.

I know what you're thinking: any sensible woman in my place would have tipped off her husband by now. *Err . . . just thought I would mention that, you know, I'm probably going into labour. Having our actual child here. No biggie. Just when you've got a minute to spare, love, okay?*

Of course, in hindsight, this is exactly what I should have done. I should have staggered down into the café, red-faced and growling, and bellowed, 'Clear the room! This is an emergency!' before Ed whisked me away to the hospital. That would indeed have been the sane thing to do.

The problem was, I wasn't fully using my 'motherhood' brain at this point. I was still in café-owner mode, thinking what a disaster it would be if Ed was called away now, when he was the only person able to cook steak and chips for the punters. I was thinking about all those hungry customers. The chaos that would ensue if we did a flit. I was thinking that Ruby Woodward's birthday dinner would be ruined, and that Betty might never speak to me again if I mucked up her anniversary night.

No, I told myself. Business first, baby second, as far as tonight was concerned. The minute they stopped serving down there, I would call Ed and we would make our move. *Sounds like you're a way off yet,* my mum had said. I just had to hope she was right.

The next few hours passed in a strange, surreal blur. I paced around. I lay down. I did my kneeling and leaning over the coffee-table thing. I watched the clock, but my contractions were still ten or twelve minutes apart. This could go on for days yet, I thought, remembering my mum's thirty-six-hour labour marathon and viewing her with a whole new respect. (Thirty-six hours of *this*! My mum was hardcore. Why had she not been made President of the Entire World for such a feat of stamina?)

When it got to nine o'clock I rang the midwifery team, just to let them know things had started. As luck would have it, Maria was on duty that evening.

'Hello, Evie, how exciting,' she said. 'Have those waters broken yet?'

'Not yet,' I replied. Another reason not to venture down to the café, I told myself. Imagine the health-and-safety nightmare I could cause! I pictured my waters breaking with the force and volume of a tidal wave, splashing diners and their plates of food. The horror of such a scene almost made me want to giggle. The café would be closed down in a heartbeat, before you could even say the words 'childbirth emergency'.

'Okay, well, keep me up to date,' she said. 'Try to rest while you can, in the meantime. You could be in for a long night.'

At long last it was eleven o'clock, and the final groups of customers were leaving the café, laughing loudly to one another as they straggled down the front steps. Thank goodness. I had made it! I was almost faint with relief at the thought that I had waited long enough, and that finally I could tell Ed the news and we could be on our way to hospital. The thought of his face – excited, nervous, perhaps a little bit scared, too – made me feel better straight away.

I was just bracing myself to move across the room – this had become a daunting prospect – when I heard Ed's voice: 'Won't be long!' followed by the bang of the back door. I froze in horror, filled with panic. *What?* I thought. Won't be *long*? Where was he *going*? Another contraction came and I found myself making the growling noise more loudly. Actually, it had become more of a bellowing moo, like no other sound I had ever made before. It was like being possessed. 'Nnnnggggh,' I mooed in despair. 'NNN-NGGGGHHH.'

The contraction passed, leaving me panting and weak. It was only then that I worked out what was going on. Of course. Ed always gave Josh and Tilly a lift home after Friday and Saturday evening shifts, to save them walking in the dark. Josh was local, but Tilly lived in the next village, a good twenty minutes away by car, even at this time of night. Oh, great. So now I had even longer to wait!

I fumbled for my phone. I had to tell Ed to hurry up. The pain was starting to get really full-on. I had lost track of how often the contractions were coming now, but they were sweeping in all the time, each one bigger and more powerful than the last. So much for my birth plan and my hopes for no pain. Ha! It wasn't working out quite as well as I had hoped.

I found Ed's number and pressed Call, hoping he would pull over when he saw that it was me ringing, rather than let it go to voicemail. It rang and rang until I heard his pre-recorded message, and I groaned in dismay. The signal in Carrawen was often bad. His phone might not even have rung, for all I knew. 'IIi, it's me,' I panted down the line. 'The baby's coming. Just hurry straight back, will you? As fast as you can. See you soon. *Hurry!*'

Another contraction came, bigger and stronger,

and I clung to the coffee table, groaning and mooing, the sound coming from deep within me. Oh, God. Everyone had told me that first babies took forever to arrive. Ha! I had a horrible feeling that baby Walnut was in a hurry to make an appearance.

I rocked my hips from side to side, then felt a sudden gush as my waters broke all over the floor. I roared as the contraction took hold, no longer sure what I was doing. I felt scared and panicky. What if Ed didn't come back for ages? What if I had left it too late? I didn't want to be here all on my own. This was turning into a complete disaster!

Then came a knock at the door. 'Is . . . is everything all right?' came a tentative voice. It was Helen. *Helen!* I had forgotten about her. She must still have been clearing up downstairs as Ed went off with the other two.

'The baby's coming,' I panted. I was aware that I was kneeling in a puddle of my own making, that I was scarlet-faced and unkempt, clinging to the coffee table as if it were a life-raft. 'Help me,' I groaned. 'Please. I'm really frightened.'

Helen hesitated, looking very much as if she wanted to turn and make a run for it. For a horrible second I thought she was going to do just that, and I opened my mouth, ready to beg her to stay. Then she came closer, still wary, but in the room at least. 'Does Ed know?'

'I can't get hold of him. I—' I broke off because another contraction had come surging in, sucking the words right out of me. I gritted my teeth and moaned, sweat pouring down my back. 'Nnnngggghhhh,' I groaned. I was pretty sure that less than five minutes had passed since the last contraction. 'Nnnnrrrggghhh.'

'Right. Okay. Let me call an ambulance then. I'll go with you to the hospital,' Helen said, taking charge. 'Ed can meet us there, if need be. Where's your phone?'

'Here,' I said weakly. The contraction petered out and I put my head back on the coffee table, feeling spent. My God, this was an ordeal and a half. Did women really put up with this for hours on end? And why did anyone ever suffer it twice? This was it for me, I decided. Walnut, you're an only child, mate. And you can count yourself lucky that I'm going through with this at all.

I dimly heard a squelching sound and realised it was Helen walking on the carpet, which had been made soggy by my waters breaking. Could I *feel* any more embarrassed? There was no dignity to be had in childbirth. Not a single shred.

'Sorry about this,' I mumbled, shutting my eyes.

'Don't you worry,' Helen said. 'I'll get you sorted out. We'll be fine.'

Chapter Eleven

Helen

Helen rang the ambulance and then Evie's midwife, trying to sound in control, although inside she was an utter stew of nerves. Of all the people to be doing this, she was surely the worst possible woman for the job. She had been tempted to bolt, not wanting to play any part in Evie's childbirth dramas. It was just too hurtful. Too much like salt in the wound. But then again, Evie was so pale and sweaty and scared that only a monster could have walked away.

'An ambulance is coming,' Helen said at the end of the call. 'They'll be about twenty minutes, okay? I only have my bike here, otherwise I would take you myself. Your midwife said she would see you at the hospital, and to ring if you need anything else. But I'll stay with you in the meantime. Have you had any pain relief? Can I get you anything?'

Evie gave a hollow laugh at the words 'pain

relief'. 'All we have here is some ancient Lemsip and indigestion tablets,' she said limply. Her eyes were glassy, as if her mind was elsewhere. 'Oh, God. Twenty minutes? Did you say twenty minutes? I don't think I can wait that long. This is horrible. It's really, really awful.'

'How about a hot-water bottle? That might be nice on your back,' Helen said. She got up, but Evie grabbed at her hand.

'No! Please, just stay here. Stay with me. Another one's coming.'

Her whole body went tense as the contraction hit. Her eyes bulged and she gave a loud, guttural bellow of pain. She squeezed Helen's hand so tightly that her knuckles blanched, and Helen's bones were crushed together beneath the skin. Feeling helpless, Helen used her other hand to rub Evie's back in slow circles, wishing there was more she could do.

'Try not to worry,' she said, as she sifted through her brain, trying to dredge up every childbirth article she had ever read for words of encouragement. Fortunately for Evie, Helen had read a *lot* of magazines. 'If the baby's coming fast – like this one – it just means that everything is working fine, okay?' she remembered. 'Your body knows exactly what to do. Keep breathing. I'm here. It's all going to be fine.'

The contraction seemed to subside again and Evie pushed her hair out of her eyes. 'Thank you, Helen,' she said in a small voice. 'I'm so glad you're here. And that thing you're doing on my back is lovely.'

'Good. You're doing really well. Ed will be back soon, and the ambulance will be here, too.' Helen glanced at her watch, praying that this was true. She was trying to act calm, but if it came to having to deliver a baby on her own, she wasn't sure she could cope.

'You won't leave me, will you? You won't go? I know we haven't got on, but please help me out until someone comes. Please, I'm actually begging you.'

The fear in her words caught Helen off guard and she felt like a terrible person for ever having thought of doing a runner. 'I'm not going anywhere,' she said quietly. 'Although I will put the kettle on for a hot-water bottle. Is that okay? I think it might help a bit. I'll come straight back, I promise.'

'Thank you,' Evie said, resting her head on her arms and shutting her eyes.

Helen hurried through to the kitchen and filled the kettle. There was a calendar up on the wall, on which Evie had charted the weeks of the pregnancy and had drawn a smiley face beside her due date. A large fruit bowl was piled high with apples, oranges and grapes. There was a pile of baby bibs on the small, round table, along with some white knitted bootees and a soft little hat. Up on the wall were black-and-white scan pictures, and there was a list of possible names, in both Evie's and Ed's handwriting.

Tears pricked Helen's eyes suddenly as she set the kettle to boil. *I know we haven't got on*, Evie had said just now, but that was only because Helen had taken against her on sight. She had put up a brick wall, shunning Evie's attempts at conversation, freezing her out. Unfairly, she realised now, with a lump in her throat. The only crime Evie had committed was to be heavily pregnant when she, Helen, had not been able to get that far. But Evie seemed a nice enough person. She was sure to be a good mother. It wasn't her fault that Helen and Paul were struggling to have a baby themselves.

Helen looked under the sink and in drawers, in search of a hot-water bottle, and at last found one in a cupboard. Before she could fill it, though, there came the sound of a vehicle outside, shortly followed by a thunderous knocking from downstairs. 'It's the ambulance!' she cried. 'Sit tight, I'll just let them in.'

Relief surged through her as she led the para-medics upstairs. Thank goodness people who knew what they were doing had arrived. 'Hello, Evie, I'm Andrea, and this is Graham,' the first paramedic said. 'Is this another contraction coming? All right, darling, hold my hand – that's it. Graham, can you get the gas and air? Here we are, lovey, have a suck on this. It'll make you feel much better.'

Helen went to fill the hot-water bottle while the contraction came and went. The whole even-ing was starting to feel a bit surreal. She fired off a quick text to Paul, who would be wondering why she hadn't cycled home yet. *My boss is giving birth! Might need to go to hosp with her. Don't wait up. x*

Paul rang back at once. 'Is everything all right? Are you sure you're up to this, Hels?'

She loved him for that – for thinking straight away of her feelings. 'Yes,' she replied, swallow-ing back her emotions. 'I'm actually fine. Kind of freaked out at first, but fine now. The para-medics have arrived, so at least it's not just me any more. There's no sign of Ed yet, but I'll keep you up to date, okay?'

She went back into the living room with the hot-water bottle. Andrea had just examined Evie and was shaking her head. 'You're not going anywhere, darling. You're fully dilated now. The baby will be here very soon. Tell me if you feel like pushing, okay?'

Evie looked alarmed. 'I don't want to have the baby without Ed,' she groaned. 'Where's Ed?'

Through the window Helen noticed a pair of yellow headlights sweeping down the hill at some speed. 'I think he's just arriving,' she said, and pressed the hot-water bottle to Evie's back. 'Hold on, Evie. Just hold on!'

Chapter Twelve
Evie

Ed burst through the door moments later, and I swear I have never been more relieved to see another human being in my entire life. 'Evie!' he shouted. 'Christ, darling, are you all right?'

But then I was into another contraction and could only moo at him, boggle-eyed, gripping Andrea's hand. 'NNNNNNGGGGHHHH,' I roared. 'GRRRAAAGGGHHHH. I want an epidural,' I yelled as the clenching sensation passed once more. 'Give me drugs. Give me everything you've got. Please!'

I dimly heard Andrea saying that she could not give me an epidural, and that the gas and air were the only pain relief they had right now. But I tuned out because all of a sudden something else was happening. A new, alarming feeling. 'I think I want to push,' I cried and grabbed hold of Ed, who was crouching beside me. 'I think I want to . . . RRRRAAAAAGGGHHHH!'

I'll spare you the rest. I'm not sure the world needs to hear the full blow-by-blow account or all the shouting. There was quite a lot of outrageous swearing and bellowing, and a very shameful moment when I bawled at top volume that I was never – repeat *never* – going to have sex again. I was in the throes of agony, so I can't be certain, but I am pretty sure I heard the paramedics trying not to laugh behind my back. Fair enough. I was glad when I realised that Helen must have slipped away without having to witness *that* particular moment.

Anyway, much as I would love to pretend I was a trooper and grimly stoic, that I kept my dignity throughout and barely broke sweat, it didn't quite happen like that. But, frankly, as soon as the baby came out and I heard Ed say, 'It's a boy. Evie, we've got a little boy!' I no longer cared about anything else anyway. We had done it! *I* had done it! Forget the stupid birth plan. Forget all my ideas. Right there in our flat was our chubby pink son – our Beach Café baby! – who had decided to be born *his* way, thank you very much. Just like Morwenna and her brother before him!

I gazed speechlessly at the baby as Andrea checked him over, my heart flooding with a huge tide of emotions. He had the most gorgeous dark-blue eyes, with a shock of wild black hair, just like me. All his little fingers and toes were present and correct, as was the most scrumptious peachy bottom you ever saw. And yes, I thought, as he scrunched up his face in a howl. He most definitely had good lungs.

I was euphoric. I was raw and bloodied and shocked at what had just happened, but the top note to my mood was pure joy. Intense, bubbling, can-you-*believe*-it? joy. Graham cleared things up around us and put the kettle on again, while Andrea showed Ed how to cut the cord and checked over our new arrival. Our boy. Our son! Then Andrea passed him to me and I was able to hold him properly for the very first time. This was it. Here he was. I felt utterly overwhelmed with love.

I put my cheek against his and he stopped crying almost at once, and began making snuffling noises like a tiny truffling pig. 'Hello, baby,' I said, kissing the end of his teeny upturned nose, and marvelling at the softness of his skin. 'Hello, little one. I'm your mummy.' I smiled down at him and then up at Ed. 'We're a family,' I said, like the big soppy muppet I was.

And then I was crying a bit and hugging Ed, and trying not to squash our newborn infant. And the world felt like the most incredible place.

After the best cup of tea of my life, thanks to Graham, Andrea cleaned up the baby and showed me how to put a nappy on him. Then – hooray! – lovely Maria arrived with her mid- wife's bag of tricks. She had found out from the hospital that we had never made it there in time, and came to check the baby for herself (and me, too) and to see how we were doing. She showed me how to put the baby to my breast, and I gasped at the strange tingling sen- sation as he sucked hungrily.

'Now there's a boy with a healthy appetite,' Maria said, stroking his cheek. 'Well done, Evie. He's beautiful.'

Once she was sure everything was as it should be, she left, as did Graham and Andrea. And then it was just the three of us. I couldn't quite believe we had been left in charge of a real-life baby. It was like they thought we were respon- sible adults or something. The very idea was alarming. What if I broke him?

'Well,' said Ed, putting his arm around us

both. 'I guess this is it, for the next eighteen years. Welcome to parenthood.'

I leaned against him. It was half-past one in the morning, and so quiet that I could hear the sea rushing in up the beach. It felt as if the rest of the world was asleep, as if we were the only people still awake. 'We really have to think of a name for him now,' I said, drinking in the sight of our baby dozing in my arms. 'I was wondering about Joe, after my aunt, but he doesn't look like a Joe, does he?'

'Max? Alfie? Henry?' Ed said, but I shook my head. Lovely as they were, none of those names were quite right for him, either.

'I want something a bit different,' I said. 'Something that really connects him to Cornwall and the café. Look at his nose! He needs a good strong name, with a nose like that.'

Ed yawned. 'Let's sleep on it,' he said. 'Maria said we should sleep whenever he does, for the first few days. The right name will come to us, I know it.'

I still felt so charged up with wild adrenalin that I wasn't sure if I would be able to sleep at all that night. Besides, I couldn't tear my eyes from the precious bundle I was holding, who had just given the sweetest, tiniest snore. I nodded, though, knowing that Ed must be done in, from a full day and night at work, followed by our epic birth adventure. 'Okay,' I said. 'We'll get back to you on the name, kid. We're working on it, all right?'

Chapter Thirteen

Evie

The next day was Sunday and, as news of the birth reached our friends and family, we were deluged by phone calls, texts and good wishes. Lindsey from the local pub sent over a bottle of champagne. Betty from the village shop sent a big shiny 'It's a Boy!' balloon and some chocolate biscuits. One of the midwifery team, Christine, popped by to see how we were doing, and told me that my GP would drop in for a home visit tomorrow. And then came another visitor: Helen.

She walked in with a bunch of white roses and a pile of post that had arrived the day before. 'I'm sorry – we were so busy yesterday, I just dumped them behind the counter and forgot to give them to you,' she explained. 'But enough about that. How are you?'

I was hazy, and wired from lack of sleep and the sudden shock of being a parent. But I couldn't help noticing that Helen was hovering timidly at a distance. She had been so brilliant the night before, when I needed her, that I could no longer remember why I had ever taken against her.

'Come and sit down,' I said. 'Come and meet the impatient, nameless baby. And thank you so much for everything you did. Seriously, thank you, Helen.' I could feel myself welling up as I remembered her kindness, her staunch heroism when I was at my most despairing. 'I'm so, so glad you were there last night.' I swallowed, feeling as if I owed her an apology. 'I'm sorry we didn't seem to hit it off in the café. I've been a bit of a control freak, I know, about not wanting to hand things over and . . .'

She put up a hand to stop me. To my surprise, I noticed that her eyes too were wet with sudden tears. 'I'm sorry as well,' she said in a low voice. She choked a little on the words. 'It was me, not you. I've been trying for a baby myself, but things keep going wrong, and I was just . . .'

Her fists clenched and unclenched in her lap; her gaze slid over to the baby, but then she snatched it away, as if it pained her to look. She took a long, shuddering breath. 'I took it out on you. Wrongly. And I'm sorry.' She reached out and stroked the baby's hair, her fingers trembling. 'He is gorgeous,' she said softly, her mouth buckling. 'I'm glad it all ended up okay.'

I felt a rush of sadness for Helen then. Sadness that I hadn't worked it out for myself; sadness that I had misjudged her and that she was clearly so unhappy. 'That must be hard,' I said after a moment. Getting pregnant had been stupidly easy for me. In fact it had been a complete surprise to us, as we hadn't even been trying. But the thought of having that denied to you, and imagining the despair and sadness month after month . . . You wouldn't wish that on your worst enemy. 'I'm sorry things have been tough.' I bit my lip, remembering how Helen had hesitated to come into the flat last night, and how for a moment I thought she would leave me to it, alone. 'And you still came in and helped me,' I said. 'That was such a generous thing to do. Thank you.'

I felt quite tearful, thinking about her kindness and that of so many others towards me in recent weeks. Then I heard my mum's voice in my head: 'All mums like to pass things on. That's just what we do.' And it gave me an idea. I hesitated for a split second, then thought, *Yes, do it.*

'Listen . . .' I said, scrabbling to reach the clasp of my necklace. I unclipped it and the silver chain coiled in my palm. *O Christmas tree! O*

Christmas tree! I thought to myself. The little silver tree had been a real comfort to me during the last seven and a half months, but maybe I didn't need it quite so much any more. 'I know this sounds kind of weird, but . . . I want you to have this. It's been a bit of a lucky charm for me while I was pregnant. I would like to pass it on to you.'

Carefully I tipped the shining charm onto Helen's palm. *There. You can help somebody else now, little tree.*

'Thank you,' she said, putting it around her neck. We both looked at it hanging there over her navy-blue T-shirt and smiled at each other. Her smile was wobbly and rather watery, but it was a smile. 'That's really nice of you.'

'You're welcome,' I said, feeling as if I was a proper mother now. Part of a club. *That's just what we do.*

Helen stood up, twitching her ponytail self-consciously off her shoulder. 'I had better get to work,' she said, with one last searching look at the baby. 'What are you going to call him, by the way?'

I rolled my eyes. 'That,' I said, 'is the big question.'

*

After Helen had said goodbye and went down to open the café, Ed set to work making us an enormous brunch. It was certain, he said, to sustain the most exhausted new mother. The baby was hungry again, so I fed him, sitting on the sofa so that I could gaze out at the beach below us, where families were setting up camp for the day. Windbreaks were being hammered into the sand. Lilos pumped up. Sandcastles decorated. Picnic blankets unrolled. Meanwhile, through the open window I could hear laughter, happy shrieks, the odd seagull and snatches of conversation from the café.

I thought about how much I loved living in Cornwall, and how lucky I was to be here with Ed and our baby. I realised, too, that I had barely given the café a thought all morning. It would be fine without me – of course it would! I thought of Helen behind the counter, looking after my customers, and I felt a twist of sadness for her again. How I hoped she and her husband would be happy in their new lives here by the seaside. I hoped, too, that some of the Cornish magic I had felt might drift their way, bringing them the joyful news they so longed for.

As the baby guzzled and gulped in the crook of my arm, I noticed the pile of post Helen had brought upstairs and reached over for it. One large, thick letter with a Welsh postmark caught my eye. Frowning, I tore it open . . . and out fell a bundle of papers. Copies of old photographs and letters, at first glance.

Tired as I was, my brain could not catch up for a minute. But then I saw one picture – of a twenty-something man with dark, twinkling eyes holding a baby in a white blanket – and I felt a jolt of recognition. Not of the man, but of where he was standing: right in the living room of this flat, where I was sitting now. And . . .

I gasped as I noticed something else. In the background was a baby's cot – and above it was the exact same shell-mobile that I had found behind our bathroom radiator. The baby must be Morwenna . . . and the mobile must have been made for her!

My heart gave a thump and I snatched up the letter:

Dear Evie,

It was lovely to meet you and come back to the Beach Café. It brought back so many happy childhood memories for me – thank you for sparing the time to chat. I thought you might like to see some old family photos, including a few of me when I was born. Just to add to your café archive! Back in the day, my dad, Jago, was

a bit of a local hero in Carrawen. Not only did
he set up and build the Beach Café, but he was
a volunteer firefighter who helped rescue twenty-
seven children when the infant school caught
fire. I know he and my mum, Miriam, would
have been delighted to see the café in such good
hands.

Best wishes for the future – and for your baby,
too.

Love Morwenna. x

I leafed through the other papers in delight. More pictures, a recipe for Miriam's famous cherry shortbread, a clipping from the local newspaper about Jago's heroics . . . So many snapshots of happy times and smiling faces, years before – in this very same place.

Above all I kept coming back to that picture of Jago holding Morwenna. The man who had built the café, a pillar of the local community. Jago was a good, strong Cornish name, wasn't it? Perfect for a good, strong Cornish man. Or boy. Or baby . . .

'What's that you're looking at?' Ed asked at that moment, walking in with a tray of food.

I smelled bacon and coffee and . . . hmm. The pong that told me our son might need a nappy change in the next few minutes. 'Ed,' I said excitedly. 'I think I've got it. How about Jago for a name? The man who built the café was called Jago.' I looked down at our smelly, gorgeous babe and tried it out for size. 'Jago. Jay for short. Is that your name? Have we cracked it, you little stinker?' I glanced back up at Ed. 'Well?'

'Jago Gray. He sounds like a really cool footballer.'

'Or a handsome actor. Or an athlete. Or an ace chef.' We grinned at each other. 'Do you like it?' I asked. 'Are we agreed?'

'We're agreed. The chosen one has a name!'

The chosen one – or, rather, Jago – finished his feed and blinked up at me like the most handsome little rascal there had ever been. 'Hello, Jago,' I said, and it sounded perfect. The perfect name for someone who had just been born in this Beach Café. 'Yes, that's who you are.' I smiled at him, stroking his soft, round cheek. There was a lump in my throat all of a sudden. 'I think we're in for some fun times together, kiddo.'

Ed took Jago away to clean him up, while I fell upon my brunch like a starving lion, thinking happily of all the fun that lay in store for our brand-new family. Rock-pooling and castle-building and wave-jumping. Christmases and birthdays. Photo album after photo album of happy times and sunny days. It was like a magical road rolling out in front of us, as far as the eye could see.

Of course I knew this motherhood lark wouldn't always feel so relaxed and upbeat. According to my sisters and every other mother I had ever met, we would be in for many broken nights and health scares, and a very reduced sex life for a while. *It's hell,* Ruth had told me, more than once.

I was up for the challenge, though. Bring it on! And if my Jago grew up to be anything like as cool as his dad – or, indeed, his namesake – then I would be a very proud mum indeed.

Chapter Fourteen

Helen

At five-thirty that afternoon Helen closed up the Beach Café for the day. There had been a sudden downpour of rain earlier on, clearing the beach, and now the air was cool and fresh. The whole sky seemed to have been scrubbed clean.

She swung a leg over her bike and cycled away, thinking about what a strange twenty-four hours it had been. Talking to Evie that morning had gone better than she could have hoped. She almost hadn't been brave enough to go up to the flat again. She'd been scared of how she might feel when she saw the baby. Envious. Sad. Bitter. What if the old injustice roared up again inside her? What if she found she couldn't say anything nice?

But it hadn't turned out like that. Evie's gratitude had been so heartfelt that Helen had softened. And then she had dared to look at the

103

baby, and it was okay. She even felt happy for the other woman. Maybe – just maybe – she was starting to come to terms with things. And maybe – just maybe – she was going to be all right.

The wet road gleamed black beneath her tyres, and Helen became aware of the Christmas-tree necklace bouncing against the hollow of her throat. Evie's lucky charm. Helen was not one for superstitions: she didn't spook at black cats in the road or single magpies. Yet somehow, today, she felt as if her luck might just be changing. Being with Evie last night, helping her when she was in such pain and distress . . . it had made her feel as if she was a good person again. As if she had faced a challenge and passed the test. And now something dark and heavy seemed to have lifted away from her at last, as if she might just have set herself free.

She turned off the road and onto the cycle path, the damp air salty against her face. What a glorious commute home this was! She would never tire of it. Already her legs felt stronger and leaner from the regular exercise, already she had more energy and slept better at night. She had new freckles, the start of a tan. There was something about being out in the sea air, too, that made her feel good. Alive again. Happy.

As she rounded the corner, Perracombe Bay came into view with its golden sands and fishing boats. What a gorgeous corner of the world this was! She and Paul had got to know a few local people now, and slowly, shyly, she was finding herself part of a lovely new community. Why had she ever doubted their move? It had been the right thing to do.

All of a sudden she could not wait to get home and see Paul. Handsome, kind Paul. Somehow she had lost sight of how much she loved him, but today she was filled with a new sense of awareness, as if she was coming out of a fog. For so long she had been blinkered, thinking only of her own longing for a child. But there were other things to look forward to as well, of course. Things to share. In the autumn they could perhaps hire a camper van and explore the coast together. They could take the diving course Paul had been talking about, have a go at waterskiing. Maybe they could even get a dog.

In the short term, though, Helen was going to hurry home and shower her husband in kisses. They would drink fizzy wine and go dancing and make each other laugh. Whatever happened in the future, they had each other, and so much to be grateful for.

She reached up to touch the silver necklace and then pedalled faster, a smile breaking out on her face.

If you'd like to see more of Evie, Ed and their lives on the Cornish coast, read on for an extract from *The Beach Café* and find out how it all began . . .

The Beach Café

by

LUCY DIAMOND

A recipe for disaster, or a recipe for love?

Evie Flynn has always been the black sheep of her family – a dreamer and a drifter, unlike her over-achieving elder sisters. She's tried making a name for herself as an actress, a photographer and a singer, but nothing has ever worked out. Now she's stuck in temp hell, with a sensible, pension-planning boyfriend. Somehow life seems to be passing her by.

Then her beloved Aunt Jo dies suddenly in a car crash, leaving Evie an unusual legacy – her precious beach café in Cornwall. Determined to make a success of something for the first time in her life, Evie heads off to Cornwall to get the café and her life back on track – and gets more than she bargained for, both in work and in love . . .

Chapter One

Family legend has it that on the day I was born, when my elder sisters, Ruth and Louise, came tiptoeing in hand-in-hand to see me for the very first time, my mum said to them, 'This is your new baby sister. What do you think we should call her?'

Ruth, the oldest twin, thought hard, with all the wisdom she'd gained in her mighty three years of life. 'We should call her . . . Baby Jesus,' she pronounced eventually, no doubt with a lisping piety. Ruth had taken the Goody Two-Shoes role to heart from an early age. Either that or she was angling for extra Christmas presents.

'Mmm,' Mum must have replied, probably in the same I-don't-*think*-so way she did through-out my childhood, like the time I told her I had definitely seen the tooth-fairy with my very own eyes, and no, it absolutely wasn't me who had wolfed half the chocolate biscuits – it was the others.

'Louise, how about you?' Mum asked next. 'What should we call your new sister?'

Obviously I was only hours old at the time, so I don't remember anything about this touching bedside scene, but I like to imagine that Louise made the little frowny face she still does, where her eyebrows slide together and the top of her nose wrinkles. According to Mum, she said with the utmost solemnity, 'I think we should call her . . . Little Black Sheep.'

Little Black Sheep indeed. I'm not sure whether this was a 'Baa, Baa, Black Sheep' reference or something to do with the fact that I had remarkably springy black hair from the word go. Whatever the reason, you've got to love my sister's astonishing foresight. Because guess what? That was pretty much how I had ended up at the ripe old age of thirty-two, with not a mortgage, full-time job, husband or infant to show for myself – the quintessential black sheep of the family. Spot on, Louise. Uncanny prescience. I was the freak, the failure, the one they muttered about in patronizing tones, trying not to sound too gleeful as my short-comings were discussed. Oh dear. *What ARE we going to do with Evie? I'm worried about her, you know. She's not getting any younger, is she?*

Hey-ho. I wasn't too bothered by what they

thought. It was better to be an individual, surely, someone who had dreams and did things differently, rather than be an anonymous, ordinary ... well, *sheep*, obediently following the rest of the flock without a single bleat of dissent. Wasn't it?

We have photos from that day, of course, grainy, brown-tinged photos with the rounded-off corners that seemed to be all the rage back then. There I was, cuddled in Mum's arms, wearing a teeny pink Babygro, with Ruth and Louise leaning over me, both in matching burgundy cord dungarees (this was the Seventies, remember), their eyes wide with what I like to think of as wonder and awe. (No doubt Ruth was already plotting her pocket-money scam, though, which went on for several years.)

I can't help thinking that there's something of the Sleeping Beauty fairytale about the picture. You know, when the fairies come to bestow their gifts on the little tot and they're all really excellent bequests, like how clever and talented and pretty she will be – until the evil old fairy (who hasn't been invited) rocks up, bristling with malice, and wrecks everything with her 'She shall prick her finger on a spindle and DIE!' contribution.

This image tended to come back to me every

time I sat in a hairdressing salon, until I began to wonder if Louise's 'Little Black Sheep' remark had somehow been a curse, straight from the realms of finger-pricking voodoo. Because throughout my entire life my hair had been frizzy, woolly and black, with a mad, kinky curl to it. Just like your average black sheep, in fact, albeit one who appeared to be immune to the powers of miracle hair conditioner and straightening devices.

And so it was that on a certain Saturday morning in early May I was sitting in a big squishy vinyl chair at a hairdressing salon on the Cowley Road, the scent of hairspray and perm-lotion tingling in my nostrils, as I pondered whether I had the bottle to get the sheep sheared into a radically different style. 'I think your face could take a short cut,' the stylist said enthusiastically. 'You've got the cheekbones for it – you could totally rock an elfin look. Maybe if we add an asymmetrical fringe – yeah. Very cool.'

'You don't think it would be too . . . boyish?' I replied hesitantly. I stared at my reflection, unable to make a decision. I'd come into the salon fired up with brave plans to request a head-turning Mia Farrow crop, but now that I was here, I couldn't help wondering if such a cut would make me look more like Pete Doherty.

I wished for the thousandth time that I had hair like Ruth and Louise – long, tawny, Pantene-advert hair, which swished as they walked. Somehow I had missed out on that particular gene, though, as well as the perfect-life chromosome.

The stylist – Angela, I think her name was – smiled encouragingly. 'You know what they say: a change is as good as a holiday,' she replied. She had aubergine-coloured hair in a wet-look perm. I really shouldn't have trusted her. 'I'll make you a coffee while you think it over, okay?'

She clip-clopped off, bum waggling in a too-tight bleached denim skirt, and I bit my lip, courage leaking out of me by the second. She was probably only suggesting an elfin cut because she was bored with trims and blow-dries. She probably couldn't care less how I'd look at the end of it. And I wasn't convinced by the 'a change is as good as a holiday' line, either. I'd spent two weeks camping in the Lake District the year before, and it was not an experience I wanted repeated in a haircut.

My phone rang as I was mid-dither. I rummaged in my bag for it, and saw that 'Mum' was flashing on the screen. I was just about to send it to voicemail when I got the strangest feeling I should answer. So I did.

'Hi, Mum, are you all right?'

'Evie, sit down,' she said, her voice quavering. 'It's bad news, darling.'

'I am sitting down,' I replied, examining my split ends. 'What's up?' My mother's idea of bad news was that her favourite character was being written out of *The Archers*, or that she'd accidentally sat on her reading glasses and broken them. I was hardened to all her 'bad news' phone calls by now.

'It's Jo,' she said, and I heard a sob in her voice. 'Oh, Evie . . .'

'Is she all right?' I asked, making a thumbs-up sign at Angela as she dumped a coffee in front of me. Jo was my mum's younger sister, and the coolest, loveliest, most fun aunt you could ever wish for. *Must give her a ring*, I thought, making a mental note. I had been a bit crap about keeping in touch with everyone lately.

'No,' said Mum, in this awful, shuddering wail. 'She's been in a car crash. She . . . She's dead, Evie. Jo's dead.'

I couldn't take in the news at first. I sat there in the hairdresser's chair feeling completely numb as memories of Jo deluged my mind. As sisters, she and Mum had been simultaneously close, but worlds apart. Mum, the sensible older one, had gone to university, become a teacher, married Dad, raised three daughters, and had lived for years in a nice part of Oxford. Jo, on the other hand, was more flighty and free-spirited. She'd left school at sixteen to have all sorts of adventures around the world, before settling in Carrawen Bay, a small seaside village in north Cornwall, and running her own café there. If Mum could be summed up as an elegant taupe, Jo was a screaming pink.

I'd loved childhood holidays in Carrawen. Jo's café was set just back from the bay and she lived in the flat above, so it was the most magical place to stay. There was something so exciting about waking up to those light, bright mornings, with the sound of the sea and the gulls in your ears – I never tired of it. Days were spent with my sisters, running wild on the beach for hours on end, being mermaids, pirates, smugglers, explorers, finding shells, rock-pooling and building enormous castles in our exhilarating-but-impossible attempts to stave off the incoming tide. In the evenings, once we'd been sluiced down in Jo's tiny bathroom, our parents let us stay up thrillingly late, sitting on the balconied deck of the café with one of Jo's special

Knickerbocker Glories and three long silver spoons, while candle-lights flickered in storm lanterns, and the sea rushed blackly behind us.

Back then, Jo had seemed like a girl herself – way younger than Mum, with her hair in blonde pigtails, freckles dotted over her face like grains of sand, and cool clothes that I secretly coveted: short skirts, funky bright trainers, cut-off denim shorts, and jeans and thick fisherman's jumpers when the weather turned cold.

As an adult, I'd loved going to stay with her too, whatever the season. Somehow, the bay seemed extra-special in winter, with the wide, flat beach empty of holidaymakers. I was there one memorable Christmas Eve, when what seemed like the whole of the village – from grannies leaning on sticks to babes in arms congregated on the beach in mid-afternoon and sang carols together. Jo brought along warm, floury mince pies and steaming mulled wine, and everyone toasted each other's good health, then a fire was lit and children danced around with red and gold tinsel in their hair. It was like being part of the best secret club ever, a million miles away from the frantic, sharp-elbowed crush of Oxford's High Street and its stressed-out shoppers tussling over last-minute presents.

But now Jo was gone, wiped out in a moment,

it seemed, hit by a lorry driving too fast down the winding lane that led to the bay. Never again would I sit at the bar of her café while she tempted me with lattes and sugar-sprinkled shortbread; never again would we chat together while the sun cruised slowly across that expanse of Cornish sky; never again would she drag me into the sea for a bracing early-morning swim, both of us shrieking and splashing each other as the icy water stung our bare skin . . .

No. It couldn't be true. It simply couldn't be true. Mum must have got it wrong. Or my imagination was playing weird tricks on me. She couldn't have died, just like that. Not Jo.

'Have you made up your mind yet?' Aubergine-Angela hovered behind me, scissors and comb in hand.

I blinked. I'd been so steeped in memories that it was a shock to find myself still in the salon, with Leona Lewis trilling away from the speakers above my head and the gentle snip-snipping of hair all around. 'Um . . .' I couldn't think straight. 'You choose,' I said in the end, my mind blank. Hair seemed very trivial all of a sudden. It didn't matter. 'Just – whatever you think.'

*

117

Matthew dropped me round to Mum's later on because I was still too freaked out about Jo's car crash even to think about getting behind the wheel myself. 'I won't come in,' he said, pecking me on the cheek. 'I'm not very good with crying women.'

'Oh, but— ' I broke off in dismay. 'Can't you just stay for a bit?'

He shook his head. 'Better not. I've got to pick up Saul later, remember.'

Saul was Matthew's seven-year-old son who usually came to ours at weekends. He was adorable, but right now, all I could feel was disappointment that Matthew couldn't stay with me. I'd managed to keep it together as best as I could at the hairdresser's – still in massive shock and denial, I think – but had been absolutely bawling my heart out by the time I got home. 'Bloody hell,' Matthew had said, his face stricken as he saw me sobbing there in the hall. His eyes bulged. 'Well, it'll grow back . . .' he said faintly, after a few moments. 'I mean, it's not that bad.'

'I'm not crying about my *hair*,' I'd shouted. 'I'm crying because Jo's *died*. Oh, Matthew, Jo's died!'

I'd been with Matthew for five years and I knew he found displays of emotion embarrassing and awkward, but he was really lovely to me then. He held me tight, let me cry all over his shirt, made me a cup of tea with two sugars and then, when I wouldn't stop weeping, poured me a large brandy too. I felt as if something in me had died along with Jo though, as if a huge, important part of my life had been snuffed out, like a candle-flame.

Guilt and self-recrimination were setting in – a trickle at first, which swiftly became a flood. I hadn't visited Jo for ages. I hadn't even phoned lately. Why had I left it so long? Why hadn't I made time? I was such a selfish person, such a rubbish niece. I couldn't even remember the last conversation we'd had, and had no idea what our last words to each other had been. Why hadn't I paid better attention? Why had I let her slip away? Now she was gone, and it was too late ever to speak to her again. It seemed so utterly, horribly final.

After the brandy had burned its way into my blood-stream, I felt an ache to see my mum, and Matthew insisted on driving me there, which was absolutely unheard of, as my parents' house was only a mile and a half away. Normally he'd have given me a lecture on the evils of short car journeys made by lazy, inconsiderate drivers, if I had dared pick up the car keys rather than my bike helmet.

But now I was here, and he was driving carefully away from me, eyes fixed firmly on the road, hands at an exact ten-to-two on the wheel, just as his instructor had taught him once upon a time. I wished he hadn't gone. I stood there in the street for a moment, hoping stupidly that he would turn the car round and come back – 'What was I thinking? I can't possibly leave you at a time like this!' – but the sound of his engine grew quieter, then faded away to nothing.

I rubbed my swollen eyes and went up the drive to the house.

Mum opened the door. Normally my mum is what you would call well groomed. She has smart shoes that match her handbags. She has a wardrobe full of tasteful clothes in shades of ecru, cream and coffee, and always accessorizes. She knows how to drape a scarf and how to do big hair, and she smells very expensive. She wears full make-up even when she's gardening.

Not today, though. I had never seen her in such a state. Her face was puffy from crying, her eyes were red-rimmed and sore-looking, with rings of mascara below them, and her hair was bouffed up crazily where she'd obviously been raking her hands through it. She opened her arms wide as if she was about to fling them around me, then froze and let out a shriek of horror instead. 'Your hair! What have you done?'

'Oh God, I know,' I said, putting a hand up to it self-consciously. 'I was in the hairdresser's when you rang, and afterwards I just . . .' My voice trailed away. Even now, at this awful time when we'd just heard about Jo, I felt stupid, the only moron in the family who'd say something cretinous like 'You choose' to an overenthusiastic hair-dresser. She'd left me with inch-long hair all over, apart from a long, wonky fringe; and yes, I did look like a boy. A stupid, sobbing emoboy.

'Oh dear,' she said. 'What a day this is turning out to be. Jo going . . . You arriving like an urchin—'

'Mum, stop it!' I said sharply, cringing at how she could equate the two things. Why did she even care about my hair anyway? It was growing on my head, not hers. And, newsflash: her beloved sister had just died tragically. Wasn't that slightly more important?

Dad was hovering in the background and gave me a warning-look-cum-grimace, so I bit my tongue and kept back the rant that was brewing inside. 'Hello, love,' he said, hugging me. Then he let go and stared at my haircut.

'Goodness,' he said, sounding dazed, before seeming to rally himself. 'Louise and Ruth are already here. Come and have a cup of tea.'

I followed him into the kitchen and my sisters gawped at me. 'Fucking HELL,' Louise squawked, jumping up from the table and clapping a hand over her mouth.

'Language!' Ruth hissed, covering Thea's ears immediately. As a modern-languages teacher at one of the posh secondary schools in town, Ruth only ever swore in foreign languages in front of her children, so as to protect them from the Anglo-Saxon equivalents. Curly-haired Thea, two, was the youngest of Ruth's three children and already showing signs of precocity. 'Kin-*ell*,' she now repeated daringly, flashing a gaze at her mum to check her response.

'Thanks a lot, Lou,' Ruth said, then glared at me, as if it was my fault. Obviously in her eyes it was my fault, for daring to enter the Flynn family home with such a ridiculous haircut. What *had* I been thinking?

Ruth and Louise weren't quite identical, but they had similar faces with matching high cheek-bones and large hazel eyes, the same long, straight noses and porcelain skin. They were easy to tell apart, though, even to an outsider. Ruth always looked as if she'd stepped out of a catalogue – her hair glossy and perfectly blow-dried, her clothes boringly casual and always spotless. On this day, for instance, she was wearing crease-free chinos, a Breton top, a navy silk scarf around her neck and brown Tod loafers.

Louise, on the other hand, generally scraped her hair back into a ponytail, although she never seemed to tie it quite tight enough, as tendrils always worked their way loose, falling about her face and neck in wispy strands. She rarely wore make-up (unlike Ruth, who'd never leave the house without a full face of credit-card-expensive slap), and had a permanently dishevelled, confused air. Her clothes seemed to have been thrown on at random – she would team a smart navy Chanel-style skirt, say, with a brown polo-neck jumper from Primark. Still, she got away with it, by being the Family Genius. Too brainy to think about style, that was Louise.

'Hi,' I said pointedly now, as neither of my sisters had actually greeted me yet in a remotely conventional fashion.

Louise recovered herself and came over to kiss my cheek. 'That's quite a look you've got going there,' she commented, her mouth twisting in a smirk. 'What's that in aid of? Midlife crisis? Homage to Samson?'

I huffed a sigh, feeling irritable and petulant. 'For crying out loud! Is that all you lot can talk about, my flaming hair? What's wrong with you?'

Silence fell. Mum, Ruth and Louise all exchanged glances, and I folded my arms across my chest defensively.

'Flaming hair,' Thea whispered to herself in glee. 'Flaming *hair*.'

'I'll put the kettle on,' Dad said, ever the diplomat, as Ruth scowled at me across her daughter's flaxen curls.

We drank tea and talked about Jo, and Mum cut us all slices of crumbly fruitcake. 'Oh, I shouldn't,' Louise said with a sigh, but managed to get through two fat wedges of it nonetheless. Then Dad produced a bottle of Merlot and we polished that off too, as the memories of Jo kept on coming.

After a while – I had lost track of time by now, but we'd somehow emptied a second bottle of wine – Ruth's husband, Tim, arrived with their other two children (perfect Isabelle and angelic Hugo) in tow, then left again with Thea. The rest of us stayed put around the table in what felt like a bubble.

'Do you remember that Christmas we stayed at Jo's, and there were reindeer prints on the beach on Christmas morning?' Louise said dreamily, her face flushed from the wine. 'And those marks she said were from the sleigh runners?'

Mum smiled. 'She got up at the crack of dawn to make those prints on the wet sand,' she said. 'But that was Jo all over, wasn't it? Anything to make the day extra-special.'

'I loved it when we were there for my birthday one year, and she did a treasure hunt all around the beach that led to my present,' I said, remembering the delicious excitement of racing across the sand in search of clues, before finally finding a wrapped parcel tucked behind a tumble of black rocks. I'd ripped it open to find a new doll and lots of clothes for her that Jo had made herself. Bella, I'd called her. Bella the Beach-Doll. Suddenly I wished I'd still got her.

'She was amazing,' Mum said, her voice wobbling. 'A one-off. And too damn young and lovely to die.' A tear rolled down her cheek. 'God, I'm going to miss her.'

Dad held up his glass. 'Here's to Jo,' he said.

'Jo,' we all chorused.

If you enjoyed *A Baby at the Beach Café* you'll love

Summer at Shell Cottage

by

LUCY DIAMOND

Sun. Sea. Sand. Secrets.

It should be the perfect holiday . . .

A seaside holiday at Shell Cottage in Devon has always been the perfect escape for the Tarrant family. Beach fun, barbecues and warm summer-evenings with a cocktail or two – who could ask for more?

But this year, everything has changed. Following her husband's recent death, Olivia is struggling to pick up the pieces. Then she makes a shocking discovery that turns her world upside down.

As a busy mum and GP, Freya's used to having her hands full, but a bad day at work has put her career in jeopardy and now she's really feeling the pressure.

Harriet's looking forward to a break with her lovely husband, Robert, and teenage daughter, Molly. But unknown to Harriet, Robert is hiding a secret – and so, for that matter, is Molly . . .

The Secrets of Happiness

by

LUCY DIAMOND

Everyone thought Rachel had it all . . .
Appearances can be deceptive

Rachel and Becca aren't real sisters, or so they say. They are stepsisters, living far apart, with little in common. Rachel is the successful one: happily married with three children and a big house, plus an impressive career. Artistic Becca, meanwhile, lurches from one dead-end job to another, shares a titchy flat and has given up on love.

The two of them have lost touch, but when Rachel doesn't come home one night, Becca is called in to help. Once there, she quickly realizes that her stepsister's life is not so perfect after all: Rachel's handsome husband has moved out, her children are rebelling, and her glamorous career has taken a nosedive. Worst of all, nobody seems to have a clue where she might be.

As Becca begins to untangle Rachel's secrets, she is forced to confront some uncomfortable truths about her own life, and the future seems uncertain.

But sometimes happiness can be found in the most unexpected places . . .

HALF PRICE

off any

Lucy Diamond

paperback in

WHSmith

3815 2122

Half price on keeping the kids amused too!

£2.49
RRP £4.99

Take this voucher into your local WHSmith

3813 7754

Book Trust believes it's never too early to enjoy books with your baby and Bookstart helps you get started. Find great ideas at www.bookstart.org.uk

bookstart
est. by booktrust 1992

has something for everyone

Stories to make you laugh

DEAD MAN Talking
RODDY DOYLE

Two women, one man...
RED FOR REVENGE
Fanny Blake

Rules for *Dating a* Romantic Hero
Harriet Evans

JOJO MOYES
Paris for ~~Two~~ One

VERONICA HENRY
A Sea Change
Something making the wrong choice is the right thing to do ....

THE NUMBER ONE BESTSELLER
Maeve Binchy
Full House

Stories to make you feel good

Stories to take you to another place

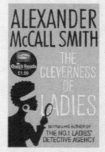

ALEXANDER McCALL SMITH
THE CLEVERNESS OF LADIES
BESTSELLING AUTHOR OF THE NO.1 LADIES' DETECTIVE AGENCY

DOCTOR WHO
THE SILURIAN GIFT
Mike Tucker

Stories about real life

Stories to take you to another time

Stories to make you turn the pages

For a complete list of titles visit

www.readingagency.org.uk/quickreads

Available in paperback, ebook and from your local library

About Quick Reads

Quick Reads are brilliant short new books written by bestselling writers. They are perfect for regular readers wanting a fast and satisfying read, but they are also ideal for adults who are discovering reading for pleasure for the first time.

Since Quick Reads was founded in 2006, over 4.5 million copies of more than a hundred titles have been sold or distributed. Quick Reads are available in paperback, in ebook and from your local library.

To find out more about Quick Reads titles, visit
www.readingagency.org.uk/quickreads
Tweet us 🐦 @Quick_Reads #GalaxyQuickReads

Quick Reads is part of The Reading Agency,
a national charity that inspires more people to read more, encourages them to share their enjoyment of reading with others and celebrates the difference that reading makes to all our lives.
www.readingagency.org.uk Tweet us @readingagency

The Reading Agency Ltd · Registered number: 3904882 (England & Wales) Registered charity number: 1085443 (England & Wales) Registered Office: Free Word Centre, 60 Farringdon Road, London, EC1R 3GA The Reading Agency is supported using public funding by Arts Council England.

We would like to thank all our funders:

LOTTERY FUNDED

Discover the pleasure of reading with Galaxy®

Curled up on the sofa,
Sunday morning in pyjamas,
just before bed,
in the bath or
on the way to work?

Wherever, whenever,
you can escape
with a good book!

So go on...
indulge yourself with
a good read and the
smooth taste of
Galaxy® chocolate.

Proudly supports

Start a new chapter

Too Good To Be True

Ann Cleeves

When young teacher Anna Blackwell is found dead in her home, the police think her death was suicide or a tragic accident. After all, Stonebridge is a quiet village in the Scottish Borders, where murders just don't happen.

But Detective Inspector Jimmy Perez arrives from far-away Shetland when his ex-wife, Sarah, asks him to look into the case. The gossips are saying that her new husband Tom was having an affair with Anna. Could Tom have been involved with her death? Sarah refuses to believe it.

Anna loved kids. Would she kill herself knowing there was nobody to look after her daughter? She had seemed happier than ever before she died. And to Perez, this suggests not suicide, but murder . . .

Available in paperback, ebook and from your local library
Pan Books

Why not start a reading group?

If you have enjoyed this book, why not share your next Quick Read with friends, colleagues, or neighbours?

The Reading Agency also runs **Reading Groups for Everyone** which helps you discover and share new books. Find a reading group near you, or register a group you already belong to and get free books and offers from publishers at **readinggroups.org**

A reading group is a great way to get the most out of a book and is easy to arrange. All you need is a group of people, a place to meet and a date and time that works for everyone.

Use the first meeting to decide which book to read first and how the group will operate. Conversation doesn't have to stick rigidly to the book. Here are some suggested themes for discussions:

- How important was the plot?
- What messages are in the book?
- Discuss the characters – were they believable and could you relate to them?
- How important was the setting to the story?
- Are the themes timeless?
- Personal reactions – what did you like or not like about the book?

There is a free toolkit with lots of ideas to help you run a Quick Reads reading group at **www.readingagency.org.uk/quickreads**

Share your experiences of your group on Twitter 🐦 @Quick_Reads #GalaxyQuickReads

Continuing your reading journey

As well as Quick Reads, The Reading Agency runs lots of programmes to help keep you reading.

Reading Ahead invites you to pick six reads and record your reading in a diary in order to get a certificate. If you're thinking about improving your reading or would like to read more, then this is for you. Find out more at **www.readingahead.org.uk**

World Book Night is an annual celebration of reading and books on 23 April, which sees passionate volunteers give out books in their communities to share their love of reading. Find out more at **worldbooknight.org**

Reading together with a child will help them to develop a lifelong love of reading. Our **Chatterbooks** children's reading groups and **Summer Reading Challenge** inspire children to read more and share the books they love. Find out more at **readingagency.org.uk/children**

Find more books for new readers at

- **www.readingahead.org.uk/find-a-read**
- **www.newisland.ie**
- **www.barringtonstoke.co.uk**